I0724994

# CHASING AMANDA

EXPANDED EDITION

THE AMANDA BOOKS
BOOK 1

ROBIN PATCHEN

JDO PUBLISHING

Second Edition

Copyright © 2024 by Robin Patchen

Austin, TX.

All rights reserved.

No part of this book may be reproduced in any form or by any electronic or mechanical means, including information storage and retrieval systems, without written permission from the author, except for the use of brief quotations in a book review.

Cover by Lynnette Bonner

Paperback: 978-1-950029-48-8

Large ISBN: 978-1-950029-49-5

LCCN: 2024913912

This is a work of fiction. Unless otherwise indicated, all the names, characters, businesses, places, events, and incidents in this book are either the product of the author's imagination or used in a fictitious manner. Any resemblance to actual persons, living or dead, or actual events is purely coincidental.

*To my parents.*
*Tex, Sara Jo, Janet, Connie, and Ray, who is still missed.*
*Most people are lucky if they have two supportive parents.*
*I've had five.*

You make known to me the path of life;
in your presence there is fullness of joy;
at your right hand are pleasures forevermore.

Psalm 16:11

# CHAPTER ONE

"So now we're going to attack a nation of innocent civilians." The long-haired English professor leaned forward and slapped his hand against the rectangular table. The man had to be in his fifties, making his ponytail more pathetic than hip.

Beside him, a chubby redhead nodded, apparently awed by the professor's insights. Opposite him, another man—this one bald, though he didn't look over twenty-five—responded to the remark with something equally ridiculous.

From his spot at the end of the table, Lieutenant Mark Johnson shot his old friend a look, but Justin just shrugged and gulped another swig of beer.

When Mark had arrived that day after twelve hours on the road, Justin had broken the news that he'd made plans for them. "It'll be low key," he'd promised. "No big deal."

Right.

Mark and Justin had grown up together. Back then, they'd both been athletes. Clean-cut and church-going. Mark still was—well, clean-cut, anyway. He needed to work on the church-going part.

These days, Justin looked every bit the Brown University grad student, right down to the bushy beard. He just needed one of those goofy blazers with the elbow patches.

Mark had never been much of a drinker, but if he was going to endure Justin's idiot friends, he might need a second beer.

The English professor continued the lecture, focusing most of his attention on his fan club, sycophants with wide eyes and slack jaws. Maybe their slack jaws could be attributed to the professor's brilliant discourse. More likely, he'd shocked them by spewing his beliefs in front of a Marine just two months after terrorists flew planes into New York's Twin Towers and the Pentagon. They would've hit another government building if not for the heroes on board that flight. Thousands had been murdered that day, but the professor didn't seem concerned about the innocent lives lost. He was more interested in placing blame—squarely on the victims.

Yup. This was exactly how Mark wanted to spend one of his last nights of freedom—listening to a liquored-up anti-American on a soapbox.

He needed a distraction.

The bar was a typical college-town hotspot, though fancier than some Mark had seen. The exposed brick walls displayed enlarged black-and-white cityscapes—Providence, he guessed, though he wasn't familiar with the city's skyline. He'd stopped in Rhode Island on his long drive back to New Hampshire from California.

The place had been about half full, the music at a talkable volume, when they'd arrived an hour earlier.

Now, college students crowded around the long bar. As their voices rose, so did the music.

Where was their server? Mark wouldn't miss the woman whose pierced face had more metal than a suicide bomber's vest.

"This whole thing was our fault to begin with," Professor Lightweight continued, loudly enough that Mark couldn't ignore him. "Those so-called terrorists are only responding to American imperialism."

Every muscle in Mark's body tensed. He folded his arms on the table and leaned forward. This weasel needed a history lesson.

But he didn't bother. Why waste his breath?

The chubby redhead said, "I'm not sure about that..." And he was off, chasing the American imperialism rabbit trail.

The professor downed the last drop of his frou-frou drink. He seemed like the appletini type.

The waitress's apron strings caught Mark's eye as she scooted behind his chair. "Excuse me."

The woman turned. Not the metal-infested face he'd expected, but a blond-haired stunner.

"You need something?" Her gaze met his, then darted across the room. Tears hovered in her blue eyes and made them sparkle.

"Something wrong?" He followed her gaze and caught sight of two men at a bar-height table near the door, staring at her.

One was laughing.

The other's mouth hung open. When he caught her looking his way, he licked his lips.

Mark would've stood and confronted them if she weren't behind his chair, blocking him. "They bothering you?"

She glanced at him again, then at the others at the table. "Another round?"

Mark heard their chorus of yeses but kept his focus on the guys paying the server far too much attention.

"Did you want another one?" she asked Mark.

"Sure."

She walked toward the bar, keeping at least two tables between herself and those men. On her way, she stopped near the front door and whispered in the bouncer's ear, pointing out the two yahoos.

The bouncer shoved his way through the crowd and escorted them outside.

The waitress hadn't needed Mark's help after all.

"...to Iraq, which was his plan all along," the professor said. "That's why they didn't stop the attack. Any excuse to get Saddam."

Mark glared at Justin. "Seriously? I'm here for three days, and I have to put with this guy?"

His friend leaned in. "He wanted to meet you." He lowered his voice. "I didn't realize... He's not usually like this."

Mark didn't bother to whisper. "Meaning he's usually a sober anti-American conspiracy theorist?"

"I work for him. What was I supposed to say?"

"'We have plans' would've worked."

"Just ignore him." But when the professor started in again, Justin interrupted. "Let's change the subject. Mark's had enough."

The professor hiccupped. "Have I offended the bellicose combatant?" He slurred his insult. "Ought I to be afraid?"

"Hey." Justin lost the placating tone. "He's my friend. Knock it off."

Mark rarely had trouble keeping his temper under control, but this guy was pushing it. A distraction...any distraction would work.

"Don't worry," the professor whispered, though Mark doubted he was trying not to be heard. "He doesn't understand what I said."

And...that was it.

Mark dropped his chair legs back to the floor with a thump that had the two sycophants jumping. "I'm a Marine, so I must be an idiot, right?"

The professor shrugged, not bothering to hide his smile.

"What do you teach, professor?"

"Literature. I prefer British, but I dabble in French and American, when I must."

"You think understanding Shakespeare makes you qualified to discuss Middle Eastern politics?"

Before he could answer, Justin jumped in. "Mark studied"—he glanced at him—"Middle Eastern history, right?"

The professor's eyebrows rose. "Community college?"

"Arabic language and culture at the Naval Academy."

"Ah. Easier to kill them when you understand them."

Mark leaned across the table toward the little man, whose eyes widened, his mouth opening in a little O. He backed away the tiniest bit, proving that even drunk, he was smart enough to be nervous.

"I believe like Shakespeare believed. 'A peace is of the

nature of a conquest; for then both parties nobly are subdued, and neither party loser.'"

The professor straightened. He opened his mouth, but he couldn't seem to think of anything to say. If not for all the liquor, he would've had a ready answer. It wasn't as if there weren't reasonable voices on the other side of the argument.

Losing his patience, Mark turned to the other grad students at the table. "History has proved that you don't get to peace unless you show your enemy you're willing to fight for it—and that you can win. The opposite of war isn't always peace. Often, it's oppression or slavery. Just ask any of the six million Jews who went peacefully to concentration camps."

The pierced server returned, the dim lights reflecting off the bolt in her nose. "Amanda said you needed another round." She handed out the drinks, careful to balance the professor's appletini as she lifted it across the table. He didn't take it from her. Instead, he looked down her shirt when she leaned over to set it in front of him.

Drunk, conspiracy theorist, pervert. The list grew.

Why was Mark trying to have a reasonable discussion with this guy and his pathetic fan club? They were already back to their stupid talk about their stupid ideas that had no place in the real world.

After the server handed Mark his beer, she laid her hand on his shoulder and squeezed. "Let me know if there's anything else I can get for you."

Mark thanked her, pretending he hadn't heard the invitation, and concentrated on sipping his beer.

Where was that blonde? Amanda, the other server had called her.

There, handing out longnecks to a bunch of guys

crowded around a table with too few chairs. She was smiling now.

She had a beautiful smile.

Most people here were younger than Mark. His friend, the eternal student, had dragged him here tonight, and it might've been fun if not for Professor Lightweight and his fan club. The bar was packed now, people filling every square inch of the place—standing, drinking, flirting. Five women—barely twenty-one, if he had to guess—threw back test tubes full of green liquid. They'd regret that in the morning. A man and woman were making out in a corner, and they weren't the only ones getting too friendly in a public place. Students occupied every stool and chair, and more lined the bar three or four deep, clamoring for drinks.

The hair on the back of Mark's neck stood up.

He scanned the room again, more slowly. There, by the window at a table for two, a young man sat alone. Hoodie pulled up over his head, yellow-blond hair sticking out underneath. Mark followed his gaze to the blond server. The man watched her as she took drink orders from a table a few feet away.

When Mark watched her mouth and focused, he could hear her voice above the din. She sounded carefree now that those two jerks were gone.

But the hooded guy by the windows was still watching.

Mark rubbed the back of his neck but couldn't wipe away the feeling. Something was wrong.

Beside him, Justin was saying, "You should see this guy in action." He tilted his amber-colored bottle in Mark's direction. "The women this guy gets. We should've all been Marines, eh?"

Mark raised his eyebrows. "That's why I joined."

The professor's skin had turned an unattractive shade of puce. Any second, he'd lose his liquor.

"It's true, right? Since the attack?" Justin elbowed Mark, splashing his beer on his T-shirt.

He grabbed a cocktail napkin and soaked up the liquid. "I'll admit women have been a bit more... grateful in the last couple of months." Mark had never lacked for dates. He usually contented himself to be his buddies' wingman and went home alone.

Fewer complications.

Justin raised his glass. "See? Still never getting married, right?"

"Unlike you. Does your fiancée know she's going to have to forever support your addiction to school?"

"Nah. I'll finish my master's this fall and hopefully"—he nodded to the professor— "be hired full-time next summer."

The professor picked up the conversation, and Mark tuned out, scanning the bar again.

Hoodie still had his eyes on the server, who didn't seem to realize she was being watched.

Then, just like that, she stepped out the front door. End of her shift? He glanced at his watch. It was just after eleven.

He looked up in time to see the creepy guy in the hoodie follow her.

The hair on the back of his neck rose again, and this time, Mark rose with it. He tossed a twenty on the table. "I'll meet you back at your condo."

Justin started to stand, but Mark dropped a heavy hand on his shoulder. "Stay. Have fun. I'll see you later."

# CHAPTER TWO

Amanda Prince zipped her sweatshirt and hurried up the sidewalk toward the bus stop. She'd recovered pretty quickly after Vince had tossed out those two perverts. She'd dealt with her share of drunk and flirty customers, but those guys had pushed it too far, one with a few suggestive and disgusting remarks, the other with an accidental touch that still had her shuddering.

After they'd been kicked out, she'd planned to finish her shift, but the manager had opted to send her home early. Kind of him, but now that she was walking on the city streets alone, fear dripped down her spine. She usually left with her fellow employees.

She'd hoped that by working at the college bar, she'd learn a little about the restaurant business—and put away a little cash. So far, all she'd learned was the names of popular drinks and how to fend off flirtatious men.

She should've found a cooking job, one that required more skill than the once-a-week gig she had teaching a family of homeschool kids how to bake. With only one more year before graduation, she needed kitchen experience. At the bar, she made more money than she would flipping burgers. But the extra money wasn't worth what she'd put up with tonight.

Nor the danger of walking in the dark by herself. She should go back and wait for her friend's shift to end.

Behind her, the door to the bar opened, and the cacophony spilled out for a few seconds.

She expected to hear voices or laughter or something, but whoever had left after her was silent.

Except for the footsteps.

She looked. One man, walking the same direction as she was.

Her heart thumped with fear. Call her paranoid, but she wasn't about to turn and walk by him. So much for going back to the bar.

She moved faster, covering half a block before the bar door opened again, interrupting the stifling silence a second time before it swung closed. Again, no voices.

She reached the bus stop, but no bus was headed up the four-lane road. Few cars were on the street at this hour. No other walkers, either, except for the people who'd left the bar after her.

A quick glance showed her there were two men on the sidewalk now. One was about a half a block away, the other another twenty feet behind him, closing in fast.

She wouldn't stop long enough to let either of them catch up to her.

She turned at the corner, crossed the street, and angled toward her apartment.

The footsteps followed.

"Hey."

She turned at the shout, the action instinctive.

Both men were closer to her than before. One wore a black sweatshirt, the hood pulled over his head—she'd seen him around campus. The other was taller and built like a pro-wrestler or something. The guy who'd asked if she was okay earlier.

Were they following her?

The second reached the first and grabbed him.

The one in the hoodie took a swing, and the bigger one blocked his punch and landed a solid blow across his jaw.

Then one of them shouted. "Run!" The command didn't sound nervous or scared, just irritated.

The guy in the hoodie barreled into the other.

They tumbled to the ground.

Shaking off her shock, Amanda turned and bolted.

<h1 style="text-align:center">CHAPTER THREE</h1>

Mark fell into the tackle and used his momentum to roll on top of the guy. For good measure, he kneed him in the ribs hard, earning a grunt, then bounced to his feet.

Apparently, the kid wasn't prepared for a fight—not one with a man, anyway.

At least the blonde had taken off.

The guy straightened, pulled a blade from his sweatshirt pocket, and lunged.

Seriously? Mark grabbed his right wrist and twisted until the knife clattered to the ground. Then he smashed his elbow into his attacker's face.

Guy screamed like a girl.

Mark swept his legs out from under him, and the guy fell onto his upper back. His shout ended with a whoosh of breath. While he struggled to inhale, Mark knelt, yanked the hood off his head, and studied him. He was older than Mark had thought. He might've been dressed like a college student, but Mark guessed he was closer to his own age, late twenties at least. White-blond hair, hazel eyes, pointy nose, and straight, white teeth.

Mark considered calling the cops, but what would he say? He had no proof the guy had meant any harm to the server. He could tell them the guy had jumped him, but considering Mark was pretty much unscathed and this guy was most assuredly *scathed*, Mark would be the one who ended up in handcuffs.

He grabbed a fistful of sweatshirt and lifted his head from the sidewalk. "If you want to live," he said, "I suggest you run." He straightened and pointed in the opposite direction from where the server had gone. "That way."

The man sucked in a breath, stood slowly, and scurried across the street, disappearing into an alley like an injured rat.

A few spectators stood twenty yards away, mouths agape.

Mark grabbed the man's knife off the sidewalk and jogged toward Justin's apartment. Much as he hated to let the little rat go, he couldn't take the chance of getting arrested tonight. He didn't have time for the legal issues. He was shipping out in a week.

The war had officially begun a month earlier. He had a week of leave before he shipped out. This stop in Providence had been a mistake. Justin had changed during his years at Brown, and Mark had changed, too. The Academy, the Marines, they'd changed him. Life had changed him.

He and Justin had nothing in common now, and after one day with the guy, Mark was tired of talking about ex-girlfriends and long-forgotten high school football games. That chapter of his life was over. Coming here had been a pathetic attempt to avoid his mother. Now that he was going to Afghanistan, she'd never forgive him for joining the Marines.

Some mothers were proud to see their sons in uniform. His mother was embarrassed. He couldn't handle an entire week of her stony stares and heavy sighs.

At least Dad was proud of him.

He slowed to a walk. Good thing Justin had given him a key to his condo. He studied the knife, still gripped in his right fist. The blade was open, the handle locked. The man hadn't flipped it open during the fight, which meant it had been open already, in the pocket of his sweatshirt.

Mark unlatched it, closed it, and turned it over. Why would the little rat have opened it already?

Mark's heart thumped.

The blonde. Amanda.

Would she have survived if Mark hadn't interfered with the little rat's plans?

He'd been watching her.

She wasn't a random target. He'd chosen her, followed her. Did they know each other? Were they exes? Or was something more sinister going on?

He dressed like a student and hung out in college bars, passing himself off as one of them. He'd followed a woman. He carried a knife.

The hair on the back of Mark's neck stood up again as he reached Justin's condo and let himself in. He had more questions than answers.

But that server had been a target, so the biggest question was this: Would the rat look for a new target, or would he find Amanda again?

# CHAPTER FOUR

Amanda skidded around the corner. Her apartment building stood less than a block away. She crossed the street and slowed to a walk, hand pressed to the stitch in her side, her heart racing. She looked up at the third-floor window above the door. No light. Was Gina home and in bed already? Unlikely. Her roommate was a night owl, which meant she probably wasn't home.

Inside the breezeway, Amanda fumbled with her keys. Her hands trembled, and she couldn't get her fingers to cooperate. What if one of those guys followed her? She turned and peered through the window in the door at the sidewalk. Empty. She took a deep breath and slid her key into the lock.

In the lobby, she ensured the door locked behind her before trudging up two flights of stairs.

Stepping into her living room, she flicked on the overhead light and dropped her keys on the table near the door. Her apartment looked just like it had when she'd left for work earlier. Two sofas—secondhand, but decent—sat catty-corner to each other, one facing the TV, the other facing the bay window that looked out over the street. The space was tidy, the throw blankets they kept for cold New England nights folded and draped across the sofa backs, as usual.

She removed her coat and toed off her shoes. She was used to being on her feet all night, but her work shoes weren't exactly suitable for jogging.

What had happened exactly? Had both of those men been following her, or was it a coincidence that they were behind her? Why had they fought?

She'd seen the smaller one around campus a few times, and he seemed harmless enough. The big one had been with a few regulars, but she'd never seen him before tonight. He was handsome, no doubt about that.

Was he the one who'd told her to run, or had it been the smaller one? She hadn't been able to tell in the darkness. Maybe the bigger one was following her, and the smaller one was protecting her. Maybe vice versa.

She sighed. Maybe what happened on the street had nothing to do with her. Maybe she was losing her mind.

She headed into the tiny kitchen and set her purse on the table. A note on the end of the counter read, *Gone with Dean for the weekend. See you Monday night.*

Monday was Veterans Day, and apparently Gina had decided to blow off Friday classes and start her long weekend early, which left Amanda alone in the apartment. Normally, she wouldn't care, but after tonight...

The more she thought about it, the less sure she was about anything. She'd felt threatened, and maybe she had been. But maybe she'd just been paranoid because of those two perverts at the bar earlier.

Whether she'd actually been threatened or not wasn't the

point. She could have been. Her parents had been worried about her working so far from home after dark. She'd ignored their concerns, but they were right. It was time to find something closer to her apartment, something with better hours and less danger.

She'd call in the morning and quit. No job was worth risking her life for—no matter how good the money was.

# CHAPTER FIVE

Mark rapped on the door of the bar at quarter to eleven the next morning. A rail-thin woman with long silky hair unlocked the door and opened it a crack. "We open in fifteen minutes."

"I'd like to speak with the manager, please."

She looked from his feet to his face. "Just a sec." She closed the door, leaving him on the sidewalk.

It was a cool, cloudy day. Mark shoved his hands in his jacket pockets and leaned against the brick wall. The blonde, Amanda, was probably going to think he was crazy, stopping by here again, but he couldn't get the image of that hooded guy and his knife out of his mind. He'd lost sleep to the images of what that little rat might do to her, what he would've done to her if Mark hadn't intervened.

Finally, the door opened again, and an older, gray-haired man stepped out. "What can I do for you?"

Mark nodded toward the door. "May I come in?"

The manager held the door open, and Mark entered. It looked so different that it could've been a different restaurant than the night before. The floor and all the brass fixtures shone in the overhead lights, and the bar and tables gleamed. Menus were stacked on the hostess's station, prepared for the lunch crowd. Nobody would guess the place had overflowed with inebriated college kids less than twelve hours earlier.

"I'm kind of busy." The manager faced him just inside the door. "What do you need?"

"Someone followed one of your waitresses, Amanda, last night, and I—"

"What do you know about it? Was it you?" The man's voice rose as he gestured toward the phone on the bar. "She was one of my best waitresses."

"She's all right?"

"She quit, that's what she is. You scared her to death. I ought to call the cops."

"Whoa." Mark lifted one hand, palm out. "I wasn't following her. I wanted to tell her—"

"Get out." The man pointed at the front door. "And don't come back. If I see your face around here again, I'm calling the police."

"I'm just trying to help. I think that guy—"

"Missy," he called over his shoulder. "Call 911. Tell them we have an intruder."

"Okay, okay." Mark backed out the door. "Just tell her to keep her eyes open. I'm afraid that guy might come looking for her."

"I'll tell her, all right." The manager pushed out behind him. "I'll tell her exactly what you look like." He slammed the door and locked it.

Mark hadn't seen that coming. Did he look like a stalker?

Right. What did stalkers look like? He had to hand it to

the manager—he'd stood his ground to protect his former employee.

Unfortunately, Mark didn't think the manager was going to pass along his message. He wandered to the corner where he and the little rat had fought the night before and looked in the direction the waitress had run. He didn't know Providence that well, but he had the general layout committed to memory. From where he was standing in downtown Providence, the Brown campus, where Justin lived, was to the east and across the river. Rhode Island School of Design was also that direction. But the girl had run to the south.

A woman rushed around the corner, the other server from the night before. The piercings on her face looked uglier in the daylight. She slowed when she saw him. "Hey."

"On your way to work?"

"I'm late." Despite that, she stopped a few feet from him.

"Can I ask you something?"

She tilted her head to the side. "Sure, ask me anything."

Whoops. He feared he'd given her the wrong idea, but there was nothing to do about that now. "The other waitress from last night..."

"What about her?" Her flirtatious tone was gone.

"I agreed to meet her near the library on her campus for lunch, but..." He smiled sheepishly. "I'm so embarrassed. I can't remember where she goes to school. I'd hate to blow her off, and I don't have her phone number."

This was a risk, too. Maybe Amanda wasn't a student at all.

The woman shook her head. "The cute guys always go for blondes. Maybe I should dye my hair."

Removing the metal brackets from her face wouldn't hurt, but he didn't say so.

The name of the campus on the other side of town came back to him. "It's Johnson and Wales, isn't it?"

"Got it on the first try." She studied him through narrowed eyes. "I'm surprised Amanda agreed to meet you. If it doesn't work out..." She left the invitation hanging.

"I appreciate your help." He jutted his chin toward the restaurant. "You'd better get in there. And, uh... Just so you know, I'm not a bad guy. I'm trying to do the right thing here."

She gave him a confused look, but he didn't explain, just jogged away.

How long would it be before she heard about the crazy man who'd been looking for Amanda? How long before she realized she'd helped him find her?

Mark headed the way Amanda had gone the night before. Maybe he could find her on her campus. He didn't think it was a very big school. With Justin in class all day, it wasn't as if he had anything else to do. He'd just warn her and give her some suggestions about how to stay safe. Then he'd know he'd done all he could.

Two hours later, Mark was cursing himself for an idiot. Johnson and Wales might not be a huge school, but it was right in the middle of Providence. There were students everywhere, along with businesspeople and families and locals going about their lives. How in the world was he supposed to find one random woman in this crush of humanity?

Cold and hungry and annoyed, he stopped on a busy

corner and peered at the passersby. No pretty blondes anywhere in sight.

What had gotten into him?

He guessed the answer, though, or at least part of it. It was the same thing that had infected most Americans in one form or another on the morning of September eleventh, when they'd watched in horror as the towers fell. As a plane hit the Pentagon, one of the most secure buildings on the planet.

All those innocent civilians—some from his own home-town—gone.

Just like that.

When he'd heard about the heroes on Flight 93, Mark had been jealous. Ridiculous and stupid as it was, at least they'd been able to thwart the terrorists. Meanwhile, Mark and his fellow Marines had been stuck on base, watching the news, pacing. Itching to fight. Furious.

Powerless.

After all his training, he'd been powerless.

Maybe that was all this was, a desire to prove he could actually make a difference. He hadn't been able to save any of those innocents on 9/11, but maybe he could save this one woman.

Fine. Not just a woman. A stunning blonde with a joyful laugh. Which had nothing to do with it.

A shop door opened up ahead, and the scent of baked goods and coffee wafted out with a couple of customers.

Food. That was what he needed.

He studied a menu displayed near the front door, then glanced inside. The place was mostly empty, but movement in the corner caught his eye.

A woman was bent over a table where three elementary-aged girls were cutting out rounds of puffy dough. Were they making biscuits?

It was the strangeness of the scene that had Mark watching. Was the woman giving the kids a cooking lesson, right there?

The instructor shifted to a different table, where an older boy and girl were rolling out thin sheets of dough. She had her own bit of dough, which she'd already rolled out. She brushed butter across it, then folded and rolled it paper-thin again. After repeating the process a second time, the students followed her lead with their own dough.

The girl focused on her work, but the boy kept looking at the instructor. If Mark had to guess, he'd say the kid had a crush on his teacher. Though Mark only saw the woman from behind, her apron was snug over her jeans and T-shirt, showing off a shapely figure.

The woman stood and shifted, and...

Well, no wonder the kid had a crush. She was stunning.

It was Amanda.

The door opened again, and a couple of people went inside and to the counter, where they ordered. Amanda paid them no attention.

Might as well wait where it was warm. Not that he was trying to hide, but he didn't want to interrupt.

He ordered a coffee and a muffin and found a seat facing the other direction. He couldn't see her, but he heard her voice as she instructed the kids. She was so patient and kind, laughing at the little ones' antics, never getting annoyed.

"Did I get these too skinny?" one of the little girls asked.

"I think so."

Uh-oh. Mark held his breath, waiting for a scolding. If

he'd been the one to mess up, he'd have been scolded or worse by his mother, and the teachers at his private school hadn't exactly been warm.

"That happens, sweetheart," Amanda said. "It's just dough. Let's roll it out and try again."

What? No berating? No humiliation? No yelling?

Not even a firm, Now what did I tell you? Try harder next time.

Not that Mark had never had decent teachers, but Amanda was more than decent. She was sweet and gentle.

The little girls were already giggling again.

When she led them behind the counter, they each carried a small tray of dough rounds. A few minutes later, they emerged with plates of steaming biscuits she must've prepared earlier.

They smelled heavenly.

The little ones quieted, and Mark figured they were eating, though he didn't turn to look.

Amanda was teaching the older kids how to cut and roll their dough. When they passed him with their trays, their sheets had transformed into uncooked croissants. They returned a few minutes later, beaming, with the baked renditions.

Now that he'd found Amanda—and had a little food in him—he was in no hurry and almost sorry when the kids' mom showed up. The kids told her everything they'd learned —the little ones all talking at the same time.

"They're so yummy!"

"Can I eat mine for dinner?"

"I'm gonna take mine to Gram!"

"Tell Dad not to forget them this time."

The mother responded to that. "I'll call him later and remind him."

Mark guessed their father owned—or at least managed—the bakery.

"Come on, kids," the woman said. "Let's go before the lunch rush."

The door opened, and then, suddenly, it was very quiet.

Mark turned to find they'd all walked out, including Amanda.

# CHAPTER SIX

Amanda hugged little Leah one last time. "I'll see you next Friday. Don't eat them all or you'll give yourself a stomachache." She lowered her voice. "And Levi will be very sad."

The seven-year-old giggled, then cupped her hands around Amanda's ear. "Levi's in love with you."

She leaned back and kissed the little girl's cheek, not sure how to respond, not that she hadn't guessed about the thirteen-year-old's crush. "I love all of you." Seemed a safe enough answer.

Friday mornings were the most rewarding and difficult hours of her week. She loved spending time with the children, but today had been especially hard, considering she'd barely closed her eyes the night before thanks to the nightmares that jerked her awake every time she did. She wasn't sorry when Mrs. Domani urged her family toward the SUV parked at the curb.

She waited, arms crossed against the breeze. Even in her navy wool coat, it was cold. She waited until the kids were in the car, then turned toward her apartment.

And slammed into a man's chest.

"Amanda?"

She stepped back and looked up.

"Thank God, I found you."

It was the man from the night before. He wore a black denim jacket and blue jeans and was much bigger than she'd realized, tall and broad and terrifying.

The sight of him brought back all her terror. She would've screamed if she could get her breath.

She turned to run, stumbling into someone's path.

"Watch it." The woman sent her a scathing look, continuing on her way.

"Please don't." The man was right behind her. He sounded exasperated, his tone familiar.

She didn't slow down.

"It's not like you can outrun me." He kept pace with her.

She picked up speed.

"I'm not going to hurt you." He touched her upper arm. "I just need to talk to you."

She spun to face him. "Why are you following me?"

Students dodged them on the busy sidewalk, muttering irritated comments under their breath.

He blinked. "I'm not... I didn't follow you."

"Althea called me this morning. My boss, too. What do you want?"

The man stepped back, lifting his hands in surrender. "I wanted to make sure you were okay."

"You mean after you followed me last night?"

"I had a bad feeling about that guy, so when he left the bar right after you, I followed him."

"Right." She looked around, searching for a friend, for someone she could call out to. "Why should I believe you?"

"Do you remember what I said?"

She thought back. Somebody had told her to run. It had been this man, she thought. Maybe.

"You remember," the man guessed. "And then what happened?"

"He tackled you?"

"Right. And you ran. And made it home safely, obviously."

She crossed her arms. "What do you want?"

"To show you something." He reached in his pants pocket and pulled out a silver object. He stepped out of the way of foot traffic. "Here."

Curious, she followed him to the edge of the sidewalk and took it. It was metal, a few inches long and about an inch wide. It had weird little holes all over it. She turned it over, but it looked the same on the other side. "What is it?"

He took the item back, unhooked one end, and flipped it open.

A knife.

Gasping, she stepped back.

He closed it, latched it, and placed it in her palm. "It's called a butterfly knife. The other guy had it in his sweatshirt pocket when I fought with him last night."

She stared at the knife, trying to process her thoughts. "You're saying...did he attack you with it?"

"He didn't open the knife to attack me. He opened it before he knew I was there, when he followed you."

She looked up at this stranger. Lips pressed closed, eyes narrowed, like he was waiting for her to get it.

She didn't want to get it.

She started walking again. He kept pace silently.

They'd covered almost a block when she said, "Are you saying...? What are you saying?"

"You need to stay alert. You'll probably never see him again—"

"He goes to school here."

"What?" He stopped again. She did, too, and looked into his eyes. They were a beautiful shade of light brown with a darker brown ringing the outside. He looked furious. "Is he a friend of yours, or—?"

"We've never met. I've just seen him around."

"Has he ever asked you out?"

"Never. He barely talks."

"But he watches you."

Her stomach dropped. "What do you mean?"

"He was watching you last night. For a long time. And then when you left, he left some cash on the table and followed you out." The stranger looked over her head, scanning the sidewalk and street around them, his Adam's apple dipping as he swallowed. "He was after you."

She sucked in a breath, forced it out. "You're sure?"

Intensity and certainty filled his brown eyes. "I have no doubt."

# CHAPTER SEVEN

Mark wasn't sure if Amanda even realized when she dropped the butterfly knife. He scooped it up and held it out to her again, but she looked past him. Her face had paled to the color of day-old snow, making her eyes even bluer. He turned but saw nothing unusual.

"You okay?"

She blinked. "I don't... I'm not sure." Was she about to faint? He thought that only happened in the movies. He reached out, almost touched her, but the last time he'd done that, she'd jumped out of her skin.

"Let's find someplace to sit." There were no benches or chairs nearby. "When did you eat last?"

She shrugged. "Dinner, maybe?"

"Okay. Food. Should we go back to the bakery, or—?"

"What? No! How do you...? I work there, so..."

"No problem. I don't live here. Where should we go?"

It took a moment, but she seemed to get her bearings. "This way." She turned down Weybosset, the street he'd been pacing for hours.

He stayed close, trying to think of something to say that would replace that terrified, confused look on her face. Nothing came to mind. When she stumbled on an edge of uneven pavement, he grabbed her arm and steadied her. At least she didn't pull away this time.

He didn't want to let go but forced his fingers to open, his hand to his side, and put more distance between them. That rush of protectiveness—that wasn't like him.

Following a woman out of a bar, just in case, then searching a city for her.

None of this was like him.

Amanda was just a woman who'd needed his help. She couldn't be anything more than that. Not that he wanted her to.

He'd had girlfriends, of course. One serious one, back in high school. A few in college, though nothing long-term. He wasn't looking for long-term. His parents had shown him what that looked like, and he wanted nothing to do with it. Especially now. He was on his way to Afghanistan. There was no place in his life for a woman.

And why were his thoughts even meandering in that direction? She was a stranger, a college student. He didn't even know her last name. He'd get her some food and be done with her.

She angled toward a sandwich shop, and he opened the door for her. Inside, he walked her to a table near the window.

She practically fell into a chair.

"What can I get you?"

She looked at the menu printed above the counter. "I'm not really hungry."

"Turkey, ham, pastrami, Italian. Whatever. Pick something."

"Turkey, I guess."

"I'll be right back." The place was almost empty, the lunch crowd gone. Mark ordered a turkey grinder for Amanda, meatball for himself, two bags of chips, and two drinks. The guy behind the counter gave him a couple of cups, and Mark returned to Amanda. "What do you want to drink?"

She started to stand. "I can get it."

"Just let me, okay? Coke?"

"Diet."

"Right back." He filled both cups, then grabbed their sandwiches and returned to the table.

Amanda was digging through her backpack. "Let me get you some money."

"It's on me."

"You don't have to do that." Still digging through the bag.

He touched her hand. "It's my pleasure. Besides, didn't you quit your job this morning?"

"How did you...?" She blinked. "Right. I'm sorry. I'm really... I don't know."

"You need to eat."

She unwrapped her sandwich and took a tiny bite.

Despite the muffin, he was starving. He guessed she was, too, though her hands were shaking so much that she couldn't open her bag of chips.

"Here, let me." She handed it to him, and he opened it for her.

Her lips turned up in the tiniest smile.

Wow.

That smile was…wow.

He took another bite of his sandwich and tried to ignore that rush of…whatever it was. Something dangerous, anyway.

"Thank you."

He swallowed the bite and wiped his mouth. "Sure."

"Not for the chips." She brushed a strand of blond hair behind her ear. "I mean, yes, for the chips and the sandwich. But for last night, for…all of it. Thank you."

Not sure what to say, he hoped a nod would suffice.

"Do you always run around rescuing damsels in distress?"

"It's a tough job." Mark shrugged, feeling his cheeks warming.

"Where's your cape?"

"Uh…"

"You know, your cape. Aren't superheroes supposed to wear capes?"

Yup, he was definitely blushing. So manly. "It kept getting caught in the car door."

She giggled, and the sound made his pulse quicken to machine-gun pace.

"Probably hard to keep clean too."

"Yeah." He cleared his throat, playing along. "Dragging on the ground all the time."

She smiled, then took another bite of her sandwich.

He watched people walking by outside. Was her hooded friend nearby? He ate the last of his sub and finished his drink.

"You want that?" she said, pointing at her turkey grinder. She'd eaten about a quarter of it.

"You don't mind?"

"Help yourself."

He pulled it closer and took a bite. After he swallowed, he pulled in a deep breath and prepared to ruin her day. "You're going to have to figure out what to do."

Any amusement she might've felt faded from her expression. "What is there to do?"

"You need to get escorts so you're not on the street alone. I bet campus security would walk with you if you asked."

"What would I tell them?"

"That some guy followed you the other night, and you're scared."

"I guess I could."

He pulled the knife out of his pocket and set it on the table between them.

Her gaze rested on it. "What am I supposed to do with that?"

"If he comes after you, you're supposed to use it."

She paled again. "I don't think I can."

He blew out a breath. She needed a plan to protect herself so he could move on.

"Are you busy tomorrow?" The words popped out before he realized what he was saying.

She tilted her head to the side. Her hair swept across her shoulder and rested against her forearm, and he had the strongest urge to brush it back.

He clasped his hands together.

"Why?"

"I'm having dinner tonight with a friend, but I thought maybe we could have lunch tomorrow."

She nodded slowly. "I don't even know your name. Shall I just call you Superman?"

He felt a grin spreading and figured he looked like an idiot. "Mark Johnson."

She held out her hand, which he shook. Small, warm, and soft. It fit against his palm as if it belonged there.

Sheesh, he was losing it.

"Nice to meet you, Mark. I'm Amanda Prince."

Prince. Princess. It fit.

He pulled his hand away and crossed his arms.

"Lunch sounds great." She dug in her backpack, grabbed a notebook and a pen, and wrote down her phone number.

He slipped the paper into his pocket. "I'll walk you home."

She opened her mouth to speak but was interrupted.

"Amanda?"

Two people approached their table, a guy and a girl, both about her age. The guy had called her name.

"And who's this?" The girl asked, addressing Amanda but looking at Mark, eyebrows raised, a slight smile on her round face.

"Mark Johnson," she said. "Superhero."

Mark did his best to look annoyed. "Just Mark."

"Superhero?" the guy said, needing no help in looking annoyed.

Amanda giggled again. "Long story. Mark, this is Sherri and Carl."

Someone caught his eye across the street. Light hair, pale skin, black sweatshirt. Watching the sandwich shop.

"I have to go." He pushed his chair back and stood. To Carl, he said, "Can you walk her home?"

"Uh..."

Quick thinker, that one.

Amanda said, "That's not necessary. I'll be fine."

Mark ignored her. "It's important. She can explain."

"I guess."

"Thanks." Mark headed for the door, saying over his shoulder, "I'll call you later."

# CHAPTER EIGHT

Amanda watched Mark exit the sandwich stop and run across the street. He paused, looked in both directions along the sidewalk, and jogged away, disappearing from view.

Strange how quickly he'd left.

Sherri tapped her shoulder. She turned and saw her friend holding out a napkin.

Amanda took it. "What's this for?"

"You have some drool on your chin."

Amanda balled up the napkin and threw it at her. "Very funny."

Sherri made a show of wiping her own chin, then slid into the chair across from her. "So? Tell me everything."

Carl rolled his eyes, sitting beside Amanda.

Sherri and Carl. Two of her closest friends. Sherri's reaction she could've predicted, but Carl looked annoyed, his lips pressed closed, his brows drawn together.

"It started last night." Amanda told them the whole story, beginning with the two perverts in the bar and ending with lunch.

"So Mark rescued you?" Sherri said. "How romantic."

"Right," Carl said, "and then he tracked you down like a stalker. How do you know you can trust this guy?"

Amanda picked up the butterfly knife—nice name for something so terrifying. She opened it and ran her finger along the flat edge of the blade. "He brought me this. He seems trustworthy."

"Seems trustworthy?" Carl repeated. "Wouldn't it be great if serial killers wore club T-shirts so we could pick them out of a crowd?"

"He's not a serial killer."

"At least we'll know who to search for when you don't come home from lunch tomorrow."

Sherri shot him a look. "Knock it off. She's scared enough as it is. And that guy was helping her, not hurting her."

"Yet."

Amanda ignored them both, carefully wrapping up the remains of her sub. Now that she was unemployed, she couldn't afford to waste anything. "I found a couple of restaurants that're hiring. I thought I'd fill out some applications this afternoon."

"I'll go with you," Sherri said, shooting Carl a look.

"Me, too. Wouldn't want you to be alone if either of those guys comes looking for you."

Amanda stifled her retort.

He wasn't wrong. She didn't know anything about Mark except what he'd told her—and that wasn't much. Maybe she shouldn't be so quick to trust.

# CHAPTER NINE

Amanda stood in front of her bay window and watched the street. What kind of car would Mark drive? A truck, perhaps? A sports car? Maybe one of those cars from the eighties with the doors that swung up.

Yeah, a DeLorean. That seemed like a superhero car. Or maybe he'd just pull up in the Batmobile.

Giggling, she peered in the opposite direction. No Batmobile. But a silver sedan parked in front of the fire hydrant, the only space available on her block. Mark stepped out and headed for the door of her building. From her third-floor window, she noted how wide his shoulders were, how thick that brown hair.

Amanda resisted the urge to hurry down to meet him. Instead, she waited until he buzzed. Then she left her apartment, locked the door behind her, and took her time descending the stairs.

Mark waited for her in the breezeway. Beneath his jacket, he wore a black cable-knit sweater with a small V-neck that made his shoulders look broader and his waist trimmer. No cape. "Good morning."

Was it too soon for his deep voice to be familiar? She felt her smile, fearing it was too big and gave away how happy she was to see him. "Hi."

He opened the outside door, then his car door. "Here you go."

Polite. She liked that.

After he sat beside her, he glanced her way, his brows drawing together. He'd called the evening before and invited her to go for a drive with him today. She'd been reluctant, thanks to the lecture Carl had given her the previous after-noon about how Mark could be dangerous, how she didn't know anything about him, how he could be a stalker or a killer. But she'd agreed.

She felt stupid for the worry that filled her now.

He must've seen it on her face. "We can stay nearby, if you'd prefer."

"I'm fine."

"If you're sure." He slid the gear into drive, checked the rearview mirror, then slid it back into park.

"What's wrong?" Had he changed his mind?

"Just giving your friend time to jot down the license plate number."

She turned around. Sure enough, Carl stood in front of the building next door, half-hidden in the shadow, writing on a small pad of paper.

How dare he? Anger surged through her, and she grabbed the door handle. "Carl. I can't believe him. Last night, he suggested—"

"It's okay." Mark rested his hand on hers and squeezed

gently. "He's just worried about you. It's good you have people who care."

She let go of the handle and gazed at their joined hands, then at his warm brown eyes. She liked the smile she saw there. His lips, the color of strawberry licorice, parted slightly and turned up at the corners. She blinked, returning her gaze to his eyes, and blushed.

His smile widened. "We'd better go before Carl decides to rescue you. Not sure I'd allow that." Mark slid the car in gear again and pulled away from the curb.

His car was immaculate. No dust on the dash, no wrappers on the floor. Not even a green cardboard pine tree hanging from the rearview mirror. It didn't need one, though. It smelled like him, all masculine and musky.

He followed a sign for the highway.

"Where are we going?"

"I thought we'd head down to Narragansett, if that's okay."

The beach in November? "Sounds like fun." Her voice squeaked, but he didn't notice, or at least he pretended not to.

"I don't want to start out on a bad note," he said, "but I have to tell you something."

She turned to face him. "Okay."

"I'm sorry I took off so fast yesterday."

"Why did you?"

"I saw the guy from Thursday night."

"What?" She stiffened like over-whipped eggs. "Are you sure?"

"He was standing in a doorway across the street, watching the deli. He must've seen me get up because he was on the move by the time I got outside. I followed, but he turned down an alley and disappeared. I lost him."

"What would you have done if you'd caught up with him?"

He glanced at her but didn't answer.

"Are you...?" Her voice was high again, like a scared little girl. She cleared her throat. "You're sure?"

"I'm sorry." He shot a look her way. "I wish I'd caught him."

She folded her arms and leaned forward, trying to stave off a wave of nausea. How had he found her?

"Do you want me to take you home?" Mark's gaze flicked to her.

She shook her head. Couldn't speak yet.

"Are you sick?"

She pulled in a deep breath through her nose, blew it out through her mouth. She did it again and again until her stomach settled. "I'm fine."

At a red light, Mark studied her. "You sure?"

"Yup. It's just..."

After a moment, he said, "Yeah." He reached behind her seat and grabbed something. "I got this for you."

He plopped a paper sack on her lap. When the light turned green, he pulled forward and angled up an on-ramp.

She pulled out a small, pink can. "What is this?"

"Pepper spray. It's easy to use. Just point and shoot."

She turned the can over in her hands. "Is this legal?"

"In all fifty states. Aim for his eyes. It'll blind him, and the pain will stop him and give you time to run."

"That makes sense."

"There's something else in the bag."

She pulled out a smaller item—a key chain. "Push the button."

She did, and an ear-piercing sound filled the car. They both winced while she fumbled with it.

Mark took it from her and pushed the button again. The sound stopped.

"Wow." Her hands trembled when she took the key chain from him again.

"If you see the guy—or anybody threatens you—use that. And scream."

"Okay."

He shot a look her way. "Do you know what to scream?"

"Um, 'help'?"

"No. Never scream help. People will either think it's a joke or they'll take it seriously and won't want to get involved. Scream 'fire.'"

"Why?"

"People like to see fire. They come running."

"So people should run from fires and run to help when someone calls for it, but you're saying—"

"It doesn't matter what people should do. It matters what they will do. Pepper spray. Press the alarm. Scream 'fire.' Okay?"

Not that it was complicated, but she repeated the instructions to herself. "Got it. And that'll make me safe?"

He pressed his lips together but said nothing.

She pulled her purse from the floor and dug through it for her keys.

"Leave the pepper spray in your coat pocket, please. It takes too long to find it in a purse. I have no idea what's in those things, but I've seen women dig through their purses for ten minutes looking for lipstick. You won't have ten minutes."

She added the new key chain to her existing key ring.

"You should always have your keys in your hand when you're on the street. Keys make decent weapons."

"I usually have them in my pocket when I'm on my way home, especially at night." She dropped them in her purse. "I assume they're okay in my purse for now?"

"You're safe with me." His voice was warm and sweet, a hot mocha on a chilly day.

She slipped the pepper spray into her coat pocket. "Satisfied?"

He smiled. "You won't need that with me, either, but better safe than sorry."

Mark took the exit toward the beach.

She wasn't the type to take off with some guy, even if he had saved her life and looked like Superman's big brother. She wasn't the girl who ignored her friends' advice and got in a car with a stranger and drove away. On the other hand, Mark had given her a weapon she could use against him. So that meant something, right? Unless he just liked a challenge.

She was being silly. If not for the weird circumstances of their meeting, she wouldn't suspect Mark of anything nefarious. He'd been kind to her. He'd bought her lunch and items to aid in her self-defense. She had no reason not to trust him.

He cleared his throat. "What are you studying?"

"Culinary arts."

"Oh yeah? You want to be a chef?"

"Since I was a little girl."

"How come?"

She settled back in the seat, relaxing. "The first time I

attempted to cook something, I wanted to surprise my parents. I was eight, and I'd overheard my father say he loved chocolate and peanut butter. I waited until my mom wasn't paying attention. Then I got out a big bowl, filled it with peanut butter, added chocolate chips, and stirred. It was really hard to stir."

His warm brown eyes twinkled. "I can imagine."

"Then I dropped the batter on a cookie sheet like mom did with cookie dough and popped it in the oven. I think I'd preheated it to two-fifty. That seemed boiling to me."

He chuckled, and she laughed too.

"My mom came in, saw what I was doing, and rescued my cookies. The peanut butter and chocolate chips had melted into a horrible, globby mess. She lectured me about how dangerous the oven could be. I was devastated. But that night, she taught me how to make peanut butter cookies.

"They were so tasty, right from the oven. My dad came in, and my brothers. They were both teenagers, and they always had better things to do than hang out with me. But when they smelled the cookies, they wandered in to taste them." Amanda could still remember how it felt having her family gathered around to eat. Not because they'd oohed and aahed over the cookies, though they had, just to be nice, but because the cookies had brought everyone together at a time when they'd all been so disjointed. The boys with their sports and dad with his work and mom with all her social functions. But for just a few minutes, they'd been a family again. Laughing and enjoying each other. "I loved that I had a part in bringing everyone together. I've wanted to be a cook ever since."

"It sounds nice."

"It was one of those perfect family moments, you know?"

"Sure." But his smile faded.

She tried to muster the courage to ask him about it. But he was so...intimidating. Quiet and tough. Older, she thought. But not too old. Not the kind of old that would make her hate herself later.

"You want to work at a restaurant someday?" he asked.

"Probably. It'd be fun to be a head chef at some fancy place. Or maybe just a little family restaurant. Or maybe I'll be a caterer. That's kind of my thing, bringing people together."

"You'll be great at whatever you do."

Maybe. At that moment, she was curious about the man who sat beside her. What made him tick? What had compelled him to step in to protect her, then track her down? Then ask her out?

The thought that this strong, handsome man might be interested in her, romantically, had her silly heart racing.

She barely knew him, but what she knew, she liked. No matter what he felt about her, she was definitely interested in him.

## CHAPTER TEN

THE RESTAURANT WAS a casual beachside place decorated
with an abundance of buoys and lobster traps and nets and
oars. The tables and chairs of scuffed dark wood matched the
floor, which felt just a little gritty with sand beneath Mark's
sneakers as he followed Amanda and the host across the
dining room. Just a few of the tables were occupied, and he
was pleased with their table next to a window that overlooked
the patio and, beyond that, the Atlantic.

They'd barely taken their chairs when a server stopped.
"What can I get you to drink?"

"Diet Coke," Amanda said.

"Water for me."

The server left, and Amanda settled in to study the
menu.

Mark studied her, fascinated. She'd read for a minute,
then her eyes would scrunch together, and a wrinkle would
appear between her eyebrows.

Was she worried about the prices?

He glanced at his menu. "Order whatever you want. I'm

getting the surf and turf." Steak and lobster. The only thing on the menu that simply read, *market price.* It didn't matter to him what it cost. He'd be eating nothing but government issued meals for a year at least. Besides, he'd skipped breakfast in a weird attempt to get the day over with sooner. No breakfast. Early lunch. Have Amanda home by midafternoon with her pepper spray and key chain and safety tips.

He planned to be done with her by dinnertime.

Except, if he really wanted to do that, he could've taken her to lunch in Providence. Even better, he could've dropped the bag of self-defense items at her door with five minutes of instructions.

What was he doing at the beach? In November?

Her hands shook as she brushed her hair behind her ear. She'd dropped her guard for a few minutes in the car when she told him about her family. She'd smiled a genuine smile, even laughed a little. But then she'd stiffened and clammed up. Now, she read the menu with those bright blue eyes as if there'd be a test later. Every so often, she'd mutter something under her breath. "The fish and chips look good." Then, "I wonder how much garlic they put in the scampi." And, "Ooh, I haven't had haddock in a long time." He hardly heard her, more interested in watching her lips move.

She was captivating.

Finally, she set the menu down. "Fish tacos."

"Seriously?" He looked at the menu and saw that it was one of the cheapest seafood items listed. "Get what you want, please."

"I want the fish tacos. I've never had them, and they sound good."

He sat back. "If that's what you want."

She sat back, too, and unwrapped her napkin, freeing the silverware and placing it carefully on the paper placemat. She draped the napkin on her lap. Everything about her was miniature—her hands, her cute little nose, even her feet were tiny. Standing at full height, she barely reached his chest. How could someone so small have such power over him?

He wanted to know everything about her. Where she was from, her favorite subjects in school, her friends, her likes, her hobbies, her favorite TV show. Everything. He couldn't decide what to ask her first. Then he remembered what she'd said earlier. Last night, he suggested... Last night. Carl.

"So did you and Carl have a date last night?"

"What?" Her eyes widened. "No. I had a party. It was Sherri's birthday."

Ridiculous, the relief that spread through him. He had to work to keep from smiling.

"I would've invited you," she said, "but you disappeared on me."

"I had plans, so I couldn't have come."

"Did you have a date?"

"No, no. Just friends." Was Amanda jealous? He couldn't let himself consider that. And he wasn't jealous, either. Obviously. Why should he be? He tapped his fingers against the table and tried to sound casual. "Carl was there, I guess."

Her face darkened as if a cloud had blown in front of the sun. Her lips turned down at the corners, and that little wrinkle appeared between her eyebrows. "Yeah, he was there."

He waited for her to explain why that bothered her. She didn't.

The server delivered their drinks and took their orders.

When she left, Amanda folded her hands again. He remembered how she'd acted at the bar Thursday night, how she'd laughed with the customers like she was comfortable. Why didn't she feel comfortable with him?

Oh yeah. Carl.

"Tell me about your party."

"It was so fun." Amanda launched into a story about the evening, about one of her friends deciding they all needed to play games, and how it was surprisingly hilarious. And there it was—her comfortable smile.

He loved watching her, the way her face brightened when she was happy. Her eyes were wide, her smile open. Her hands joined the conversation, moving, flipping, pointing. She was so innocent.

She stopped, and her hands settled on the table. "Innocent?"

Oops. "Did I say that out loud?"

"Uh-huh."

"Sorry. But it's true. Your innocence is..." He grasped for a word. Sweet, refreshing, enchanting. "I like it."

Her lips turned down in a full-fledged frown. She crossed her arms. "I'm not that innocent."

"I meant it as a compliment."

"You didn't mean to say it. And I'm just saying, I don't want you to think I'm something I'm not."

"I didn't mean to offend you. I think it's beautiful. You're beautiful."

She looked away, sipping her Diet Coke.

"Sorry," he said, though he wasn't sure why he should be. "I like your enthusiasm, the way you don't hide your feelings or act like everything has to be a mystery."

She looked at him again, head tilted to the side. Her hair pooled around her shoulder. Without thinking, he reached across the table and brushed it back, tugging a strand gently, enjoying the silky feel of it.

She shivered and blushed.

He shouldn't have done that. "So, are you from around here?"

"Are you asking me if I come here often?" She grinned, shaking her head. "Natick, Mass. You?"

"Little town near the New Hampshire coast."

"You moved farther from home than I did. What were you doing at the bar last night?"

"Drinks with a friend. He's a graduate student at Brown."

"And what do you do?"

He took a long sip of his soda. He didn't want to tell her what he did, who he was. Not yet. He wasn't prepared for her reaction, whatever it might be. He hated when people treated him like the professor had the other night, as if being a Marine meant he liked killing people. Not that he'd ever killed anyone, though the thought had crossed his mind with Amanda's stalker.

But that reaction he could handle. People like the professor could be brushed off.

His mother was ashamed of him. He felt that sometimes, like his existence embarrassed people. He was used to dealing with that.

It was the ones who treated him as if he'd done something gallant by joining the Marines. As if it made him a hero.

Mark didn't feel like a hero, never had. He'd joined because it was all he'd ever wanted to do. Now his country was at war, and he was prepared to do what he'd been trained to do.

He didn't want to think about it. And he certainly didn't want Amanda to know. Not yet.

How would she react? Would she be proud of him? Angry he hadn't told her earlier? Would she be disgusted?

What would that look like on her perfect face?

He'd paused too long.

Her head tilted to the side, and her mouth turned down in a frown. "Are you a student too?"

"Graduated a few years back," he said, thankful for the out. "I'm probably too old for you."

She uttered a dark chuckle he didn't understand. "I doubt it. How old are you?"

"Twenty-seven. You?"

"Twenty-one. See, just six years."

She said it as if it were great news, as if there were no barriers between them that couldn't be crossed.

What was he doing?

Falling for her.

What in the world?

He'd just met this woman. He barely knew her. She didn't know him at all.

Somehow, he was falling for a twenty-one-year-old college student who had no business wasting her time with a Marine headed off to war.

If only he had the strength to end it before it went too far.

# CHAPTER ELEVEN

Amanda picked at the fish tacos. How could she eat with Mark sitting across from her? This handsome, kind, heroic man who couldn't take his eyes off her? Was he just a charmer? Maybe he did this all the time. She might believe that except he wasn't exactly smooth. Actually, he was a little awkward, saying things he didn't mean to say, like when he'd dropped that innocent comment earlier.

Mark was telling her about his friend in Providence, an old friend from his hometown, and the restaurant they'd gone to the night before. Mark had met Justin's fiancée for the first time at dinner. Amanda hadn't ever been part of an official couple. Had Mark?

She really wanted to know. When he finished his story, she gathered her courage. "Have you ever had a serious girlfriend?"

"In high school. We were pretty serious, but then she moved to New York, and I went to college."

"What was she like?"

"She was sweet."

He cut a piece of his steak, popped it in his mouth.

"Do you miss her?"

He swallowed. "Uh, no. Not at all. It felt real in high school, but..." He shrugged. "We would never have made it. We're too different."

"Is she still in New York?"

"I assume, mostly. I think she travels for work. How about you? Serious boyfriends?"

"Not really. There was one guy in high school. Like you, it seemed serious at the time, but in retrospect..." She let her words trail off. No way was she getting into that with Mark. With anybody.

"I can't believe any guy was dumb enough to let you go."

She picked at the fish, flaked it into tiny pieces. "It's not that shocking."

He reached across the table and slipped his hand over hers, the feeling warm and comfortable, as if they'd been holding hands forever. He said nothing, just watched her.

And she knew.

All those stories about love at first sight, about how people knew from the very first look—or the first date, anyway—that they were meant to be with someone.

She'd scoffed at those stories, but now... Now, she got it.

She and Mark were together. Somehow, she knew they would be together forever.

Heat filled her cheeks, and she dropped her gaze before he noticed, focusing on their joined hands. What a silly, stupid notion. Thank heavens he couldn't read her mind. He'd probably think she was nuts.

But even if it was crazy, it felt right. Not that her feelings were any barometer of truth—she'd learned that the hard way. But there was something about Mark that connected with something in her. Or maybe it was everything about him connecting with everything in her.

They were good together. They were meant to be together.

She steeled her courage and looked up.

He held her eye contact, and all her crazy feelings were right there, between them. As if he could read her mind. Or maybe he was having the same thoughts.

And then he blinked. His expression shuttered, and he yanked away and pushed back from the table. "Sorry. I'll be…"

He fled out the door, leaving her with an icy hand and half-eaten fish tacos, wondering what had just happened.

# CHAPTER TWELVE

Mark might as well have run screaming from the restaurant.

He welcomed the stiff wind blowing off the Atlantic. Maybe it would cool things off a little.

This was crazy. How could he fall in love in...what? Twenty-four hours? Thirty-six, if he started counting when he'd first laid eyes on her. Who did that?

It didn't even make sense, especially not for Mark, who'd sworn since he was eleven years old he would never, ever fall in love. He'd broken that rule once and paid the price. He had no intention of doing it again. No intention of getting married and saddling himself with some woman who'd turn into an angry, bitter shrew.

He had quite enough *shrew* already in his mother.

And yet, here he was, tumbling through some rabbit hole like Alice-in-flipping-Wonderland. Except Alice had probably been suffering a psychotic break.

Was falling in love all that different, really? He was losing his head, losing his heart, losing his ever-loving mind.

This was the terrorists' fault. He blamed them and the attacks two months before. Now that America was at war, his feelings were heightened. Not just his, either, he didn't think. The good seemed amazing, the bad horrendous, the future uncertain. Why not fall in love?

He could think of a few reasons. Well, he *would* think of them, if it weren't already too late.

That was the problem, of course.

It was too late.

Whatever.

It was one thing for Mark to fall for Amanda. To bring himself pain. Stupid, definitely. It certainly wouldn't help him climb on that plane in a week. But having Amanda on his mind while he was fighting—he could think of worse images to focus on. Now that he'd spent so much time with her, he'd be able to pull out his memories like photographs whenever he was lonely. He'd remember her smile, her voice, her laugh. This weekend could carry him through the war.

But she wasn't supposed to know how he felt. Somehow, she'd picked up on it. Somehow, she felt it too.

She was a student with better things to worry about than some Marine halfway around the world.

He had to stop this before it got out of control.

He had to tell her the truth. And he needed help to do it because the last thing he wanted was to hurt her.

Mark had gone to church as a kid, but he hadn't had a lot of time for God in the last few years. Sure, he'd done a good thing rescuing Amanda the other night. And going into the service—that had to count for something. But would those good things make up for all the bad? Would they make up for all the ways he'd disappointed his mother? For his short-coming and sins? For breaking Amanda's sweet heart?

He gazed up at the clear blue sky. "Help me out here, God. Tell me how to do this."

Not that he'd expected a voice or anything, but he'd hoped for some insights or something. He got nothing, though, and a few minutes later, he gave up and made his way back inside.

She watched him, wariness in her gaze, as he made his way to their table and slid in across from her.

"Sorry about that."

"It's fine." But in those two words, he knew she'd lifted her defenses again.

Probably just as well. "Are you finished?"

"Uh-huh. You?"

He dropped more than enough money on the table without waiting for the check. "Let's go."

He placed his hand on the small of her back and felt warmth through her thin sweater as he led her through the dining room and into the cool November day. Outside, she stopped and slipped on her wool coat.

"Do you mind if we go for a walk?" he asked.

"Fine."

They made their way across the street and onto the side-walk that ran the length of the beach. He walked at a slow pace, adjusting to her shorter legs. Empty benches lined the lane every twenty or thirty feet. They were alone, and it was time to tell her the truth. How could she possibly understand loss, understand the kinds of sacrifices he was about to make? How could she understand what being with him would cost her? She couldn't, and he didn't want her to. This was the only way.

"This has been fun," he said. "We should head back soon."

"If you say so."

"I'm sure you have better things to do than hang out with me."

She didn't respond. She wasn't going to make this easy.

"I love the beach," he said. "It's always made me feel connected, somehow."

"To?"

He shrugged. "God, I guess. Do you believe in God?"

"I try not to think about God."

"That's a strange thing to say."

She looked down, picked at some lint on her black coat.

"Any particular reason?"

She sighed. "When I was fifteen, I was in a pretty terrible car accident."

"Oh." He hadn't expected that. "Want to tell me about it?"

She took a few steps before she spoke, her focus on the ground. "I was with my best friend and her family, sitting in the backseat between her and her brother. A truck lost control and hit us."

Her words were automatic, as if she'd told the story a million times, or maybe she was trying to keep her emotions in check. His body tensed as he waited for the rest. "What happened?"

"The truck driver died. My friend and her family died. I was the only survivor."

Oh, man. And here he'd thought her too young to understand loss. He faced her. "I'm sorry. I can't imagine."

She crossed her arms and looked beyond him, out to sea. "It changed everything, you know? I didn't understand why I didn't die too. I thought maybe God had spared me for a reason, but then..."

Her voice trailed. He desperately wished he could read her mind. "Please tell me."

She shook her head. "I guess it affected me. I started to think my plan to be a chef was stupid, like I had to do something more worthwhile with my life. Be a nurse or something. But I can't stand the sight of blood, and I have few skills outside the kitchen." She tried to smile as if it didn't matter, but tears dripped down her face.

He brushed them away with his fingertip, then stroked her hair. "Go on."

She looked at the ground. "I was messed up. I went to see a shrink. Did some really stupid things. I wanted to understand, to make it mean something. But...but it didn't. It doesn't. I can't be... I don't know what I'm supposed to be. I gave up trying to figure it out. Gave up on God. If there is a God, He let my best friend die. He let all those people die. He let my childhood die."

Wow. He didn't know what to say. Everything that came to mind sounded stupid, so he just took her hands and squeezed.

She looked up, and her eyes widened. "I can't believe I just told you that." Her cheeks turned a deep shade of pink. "I never tell that story. Sherri doesn't even know. Carl doesn't. Not even my roommate. What's wrong with me?" She pulled a hand away and swiped at fresh tears. "I don't know anything about you. I don't know where you live or what you do or where you went to school, and here I am, baring my soul. You probably think I'm crazy."

Crazy?

No.

Wounded. And precious and hurt and vulnerable and young and...

And wow, he wanted to kiss her.

*Don't do it.* But he leaned forward. "I think you're beautiful." He brushed his lips against hers.

The slightest touch, and... aw, man. He shouldn't have done that.

Electricity zinged through him. Power. Or maybe it was weakness.

She gasped. But she didn't back away.

No. She leaned in.

He kissed her again, tasting her tears.

She slid her hands over his shoulders, her fingers sliding against the back of his neck.

He groaned—aloud? He had no idea as he wrapped his arms around her back and pulled her close. Closer, diving in. Tasting everything he'd always wanted. Everything he'd never known he was missing.

Too soon, but somehow also too late, he forced himself to stop.

He couldn't bring himself to let her go. Not yet. Just gazed down at her, this beautiful woman gazing up at him with wide blue eyes.

Her cheeks were still pink, but she smiled. He rested his forehead against hers, knowing the answer to her question. Knowing exactly why she'd been spared in that car accident.

For him.

No.

It took all his strength, but he stepped away from her. "I'm glad you told me. About the accident. That must've been... I can't imagine."

He sounded like an idiot.

She closed her eyes.

He took her hand and started walking again. Forcing himself to take his eyes off her so he could think straight.

All he wanted to do was kiss her again.

He'd tell her now, and it would all be over.

His gut did a weird wrenching thing, like something was ripping apart in there. And something was. His heart.

"What?" Her question was soft, almost fearful.

He looked at her, saw her studying him, and looked away. "I didn't say anything."

"It's written all over your face. You're upset. You're sorry you kissed me."

He pulled in a deep breath and pushed it out. "I shouldn't have done that."

Tears pooled in her eyes.

Nice. Make her cry. What was wrong with him? "I'm sorry. Please don't be offended. I've spent the last few years of my life trying very hard not to get involved with anyone, and now with just a week left..."

He hadn't meant to say it that way. Man, he was screwing this up.

"A week left until what?" She squeezed his hand and smiled, though it was slight. "Do you have to go back to Krypton?"

Superman again. She wouldn't think that much longer.

"I'm being deployed in a week."

She stopped. "Deployed?" The pitch of her voice rose to a near squeak. "What do you mean?"

"I'm a Marine, Amanda. I'm going to Afghanistan."

Her breath whooshed away as if she'd had the wind knocked out of her. She rested her hand over her heart. "Oh. That's...no." She wiped away fresh tears and turned toward the beach. "I should've... Of course."

When she said nothing else, he asked, "Are you okay?"

She shook her head.

He led her to a bench about ten feet away. They sat beside each other. "I'm sorry. About all of this. I should've just handed you the sack with the stupid pepper spray and key chain and taken off."

Tears trickled down her cheeks. "Why would you say that? You're sorry you kissed me. Now you're sorry we got to know each other. Are you sorry you met me, too? Sorry you followed me out of the bar the other night?"

A wave of frustration colored his tone. "If I hadn't followed you—"

"Maybe you're sorry about that, too."

"Don't be ridiculous." He forced himself to soften his tone. "I'm not really sorry about any of it, except now that I've met you, I don't want to leave. And I certainly don't want you worrying about me, like there's some..." He let his voice trail off.

She crossed her arms. "Some what?"

"Some future for us or something. I'm going to war."

She shifted on the bench and stared into his eyes. He wouldn't look away. He couldn't let her see his wavering emotions, the pain he was feeling. She'd be better off with a clean break.

"You leave in a week?" she asked.

He shrugged. "Something like that."

"So we have a week."

"No, we don't."

"You just said—"

"I'm just here for a visit. I'm leaving tomorrow. I need to spend some time with my parents—"

"Why aren't you home when you're about to go to war?"

"A week with my mother is... You'd have to know her to understand."

She lifted her eyebrows.

"She hates that I'm a Marine. She'll never forgive me for getting sent to war."

"I'm sure she's just worried about you."

"Hmm." No sense trying to explain to someone like Amanda. She obviously had a healthy family.

"And it's not like you have a choice."

He shrugged. "Even if I did—"

"You'd go?"

He nodded but said nothing.

And then, for no good reason, Amanda smiled. "Okay."

"Okay?"

She stood and walked along the sidewalk toward his car. "If this is going to be the only day we get to spend together, let's make the best of it."

He caught up with her, pretending he didn't feel a little jolt of excitement, knowing she still wanted to be with him.

Regardless of how they felt today, he'd still be leaving her.

How could they make the best of it? Because leaving her—
that might be the hardest thing he'd ever have to do.

# CHAPTER THIRTEEN

Amanda led the way to the parking lot where they'd left Mark's car. "Where should we go?"

"I should just take you home."

She stopped on the sidewalk and stared at him.

He crossed his arms, not smiling. A battle raged behind his eyes. He didn't want to take her home.

She'd never been so certain about anything in her life. And that was good, because she couldn't bear to think about being separated from him until it was absolutely necessary. "We're not going to worry about what you think you should do, okay?"

She could invite him to her apartment, but she feared he really would drop her off and leave. "There's a mall in Warwick. Do you like shopping?"

"I hate it."

"Me too. Let's go."

. . .

IT WAS A TYPICAL MALL. One story, bookended by department stores with specialty shops scattered in between, decked out for Christmas, despite the fact that Thanksgiving was still a couple of weeks away. They walked from one end to the other while Amanda peppered Mark with questions. They'd covered the basics, but she wanted to know everything.

"In the car on the way to lunch, when I told you about the peanut butter cookies, you had a funny look on your face. Did your mother not bake? Or was it something else?"

Mark chuckled, but the sound held no joy. "It's not good that you can read me so easily."

"Oh, I don't know." She stopped and looked up at him. "Can you read me?"

He studied her for so long that her cheeks burned. Finally, he smiled. "Like a children's book."

"Maybe that's the way it's supposed to be."

His lips tipped up, almost a smile, and she knew he felt it, too, this thing between them.

He started walking again. Neither one of them had so much as glanced into the stores. "I'm an only child. Unfortunately, my parents don't like each other very much. We had few happy family moments."

She squeezed his hand. "That must've been hard."

Mark steered her toward the food court and the scent of greasy hamburgers and gooey cinnamon rolls, but so soon after lunch, nothing about it smelled appetizing. After he bought them each a soda, they wandered toward Macy's, hand-in-hand. "Earlier, you avoided telling me where you went to school. How come?"

"I went to the Naval Academy."

"Oh."

He swirled his drink and shook the crushed ice.

She should've guessed. His crew cut, his muscles, even the way he carried himself—they all screamed military. "It's hard to get into the Naval Academy, isn't it?"

He shrugged. "There are a lot of steps."

"Did you always want to go there?"

Mark steered her toward a seating area outside the department store, where they settled side-by-side on an industrial couch.

She put her back to the arm of the chair so she could face him.

He propped an ankle on the opposite knee, then balanced his cup on his thigh, apparently not feeling the condensation that dripped onto his jeans. "I've wanted to be a Marine as long as I can remember."

"How come?"

"Dad served in Vietnam. My uncle served in Korea, and my grandfather served in Europe. His division liberated a concentration camp."

"A family legacy."

Mark shrugged. "Didn't have to be. Dad was always very clear about that—that I should follow God's plan for my life." He watched her for a reaction, but she wasn't sure what she was supposed to say.

"My parents talk like that too. Like God has some grand plan, and I'm supposed to follow it."

"You don't believe it?"

"I didn't, but..." But meeting Mark, the way it happened, the way he'd saved her? She was coming around.

He looked down almost fast enough to hide his smile, maybe reading her mind. "Anyway, none of them—Dad, my uncle, Grandpa—none of them talked about the battles they fought. Even when they didn't know I was listening—I was bad about pretending to go to bed but listening on the stairs." He lifted his shoulders in a little self-effacing shrug. "I guess I was nosy."

She imagined a smaller version of Mark, eavesdropping on the grownups, and smiled.

"Even when they were alone," he continued, "they'd trade funny stories about their time overseas, but never anything serious. Not that I realized it. But when I was in high school, my history teacher showed a video of the liberation of Dachau. At first I was searching the soldiers' faces for my grandfather. And then, I saw the prisoners, and I was..." He swallowed and stared out at the mall. "All those people. Innocent men and women. Children. Nothing but skin and bones. Most of them had no clothes. They were treated like animals, and I just...I thought there could be no more noble pursuit than to fight for people who couldn't fight for themselves."

Wow.

He kept surprising her, this man. The more she knew about him, the more she loved him. "That's amazing."

He faced her. "Not really. You know how idealistic kids can be."

"I have a feeling you're no less idealistic today. You just hide it better."

He didn't argue, just sipped his drink. "My mother wanted me to go to Princeton, her alma mater. I applied and got accepted. I didn't even tell her I was applying to the

Academy at first. She was..." His lips tightened into a thin line. "Disappointed."

Amanda wondered what it would be like to have parents like that. "You'd think she'd have been proud."

He lifted a single eyebrow. "Only if you'd never met her."

Amanda would've laughed if not for his dead-serious tone. "But she married a soldier. She must've thought that was noble enough at the time."

"I was almost nine pounds when I was born...six months after the wedding."

"Nine pounds?" Yikes. And then the rest of what he'd said registered. "Oooh."

"Dad had just returned from Vietnam, Mom was in her probably five-minute rebellious stage. It was the seventies."

What a messy family. She hated that for Mark. Yet, look how well he'd turned out. Noble and brave and kind.

People walked by as if it were any normal Saturday. Teenagers flirting and giggling. Old folks in sneakers, getting their exercise.

But this man would be at war, like his father before him. What would he endure? Would it be so awful that he'd avoid talking about it, even with other veterans? Would he keep it from her?

Amanda didn't want to think about it. She didn't want to consider him leaving for Afghanistan. She didn't want to think about the enemies he'd face over there.

He dropped his foot on the floor and leaned toward her. "What is it?"

"Nothing."

With his thumb, he rubbed the space between her eyebrows. "Tell me, please."

"I don't want you to go."

He dropped his hand to his lap. "Ah."

"You want to go, though."

"I did. I do." He faced forward again. "It's what I've trained for, what I've waited my whole life to do." The way his lips turned down at the corners told a different story.

She wanted to press him, to get him to tell her what he was really thinking. Instead, she asked, "How long?"

"At least a year."

"I can handle a year."

He shrugged as if it didn't matter. "Probably two, maybe more. And anyway, I'm based at Pendleton, in San Diego. By the time I get back, you'll have forgotten all about me."

Forget about him? And here he'd claimed he could read her like a book.

# CHAPTER FOURTEEN

When Amanda changed the subject from Mark's deployment, he didn't complain. He didn't want to think about what was coming—and what he'd be leaving behind.

He'd known since the morning of September eleventh that he'd be sent overseas. Even before the second plane hit, before it was a confirmed terrorist attack, he'd known he was destined for battle. He'd known the same way he'd known, when he was a kid, that he was meant to be a Marine.

And not for one second had he been sorry he'd followed the path he was on. He'd looked forward to it, in fact. Maybe foolishly, maybe stupidly, he'd looked forward to putting his training to the test.

He'd never had a single reservation. Until today.

Spending time with Amanda, this beautiful, amazing woman he would never have met—maybe should never have met—if not for the strangest of circumstances.

But he discarded that idea. Of course he was supposed to meet Amanda. The same knowing that had prompted Mark to join the Marines had led him to save her life two nights before.

Which told him that there was a plan—a plan much bigger than he could comprehend. And if there was a plan, then there had to be a Planner. Mark had always believed in God in sort of an *out there* kind of way. But maybe God was more involved in people's everyday lives than Mark had ever realized.

Maybe he ought to figure out what else God had in store.

But today was for savoring his short time with Amanda.

Hand in hand, they wandered in and out of stores, not really shopping, just talking, sharing stories and histories and dreams. Asking a million questions and laughing and just... being together. Somehow, it was as if they'd always known each other.

They found a restaurant and ate dinner, then moved into the bar, where he nursed a beer while she sipped Diet Coke.

She was in the middle of a story about her older brother when she hid a yawn behind her hand.

He glanced at his watch—just after nine o'clock. "You haven't been sleeping well." Considering a stalker had followed her two days before, it seemed like a good guess. Especially since she'd told him her roommate was gone for the weekend.

"I'm fine." She sat up straighter as if trying to prove she wasn't sleepy.

"I haven't slept well, either." He gripped his empty glass, seeing her stalker, wishing he'd taken his chances and called the police. At least they'd have the little rat's name. Maybe he'd move on from her. "If I hadn't seen him follow you... If I'd been distracted for ten seconds..."

Amanda slid her fingers around Mark's hands and. "You did see, though. I'm safe."

He managed a smile, but visions of her stalker were burned into his brain. How much worse must it be for her?

Maybe Carl would protect her.

That wrenching thing in his stomach was back.

They talked until the server dropped their bill and told them it was closing time.

Five minutes after they got on the road, Amanda rested her head against his shoulder and fell asleep. He hadn't so much as twitched in twenty minutes.

He pulled onto her street and parked in front of the fire hydrant, the only available spot, thinking she'd wake up when the car stopped. She didn't, though. Even after he shifted, resting her head against the armrest, she continued to sleep. He watched her a few moments, mesmerized by how beautiful she was. How trusting.

He slipped out of the car, closed the door as quietly as he could, and walked around to the passenger side, where he opened her door and crouched beside her.

"Amanda?"

She stirred.

"You're home."

Her eyes opened, and she smiled. Then the smile faded. "I fell asleep? Oh, no. I wasted all that time. I'm so sorry."

"Don't be." He stroked her hair. "You were exhausted. Come on."

Mark helped her onto the sidewalk. "You have the bag I gave you?"

"In my purse." At the bottom of the steps leading to the

door to her building, she faced him, grabbing his other hand. "You're coming upstairs, right? For dessert?"

Desire flared inside him, and he stepped back. "That's not a good idea."

Her head tilted to the side. She looked confused and hurt, blinking those pretty blue eyes. "Why not?"

"I'd love to. I mean, I'd really... You have no idea. But you'd regret it in the morning. Or, after, you know?" He sounded like an idiot, but surely, she understood what he was saying. "I don't want to leave you with that. That's the last thing I want for you."

Her eyes widened, and even in the faded glow of the streetlights, he could see her face redden. "No, I meant... I have some leftover cheesecake."

"Oh." He blew out a breath, stepped toward her again, and rested his forehead on hers. "Oh. Wow. Okay." He chuckled. "You're so innocent. You should know, for next time, that when you invite a guy up to your room this late, he's not thinking about cheesecake."

"That's good to know." She backed away and looked up at him, her lips lifting at the corners. But the smile faded. "What do you mean, next time?"

"I'm going to be gone for a long time, Amanda. You might change your mind."

"I'm a very patient person. I can handle it."

"You shouldn't have to, though. When I come home"—if I come home—"we can see how we both feel. But until then—"

"Are you going to be dating other women?" She gave him a look—eyebrows hiked, chin lowered, that told him she already knew the answer.

"That's different. I dated a lot when I was in college. You should too."

"I don't want to, and you can't make me." The tone—half petulant, half joking—made him smile.

"You're very stubborn."

She stepped into his space and laid her hands on his chest. "Said the pot to the kettle."

He used to be stubborn. He'd been rejecting women for years, women a lot stronger and more forward than this one.

He should end this with Amanda right now. It would be the kinder thing to do.

But to know that while he fought, she would be waiting for him? What better incentive could he have to come home?

Her hands slid around his neck, and he surrendered to her. Surrendered to everything he'd never admitted he always wanted.

He bent low and took her in his arms and pressed his lips to hers. He was careful, gentle, and their kiss was warm and slow, as if they had all the time in the world.

As if he weren't going off to war. As if his life wouldn't be on the line.

It was full of promises he'd never planned to make, not to Amanda or any woman. She was kind and gentle, melting in his arms, trusting him. Trusting him to be true to her. Trusting him to protect her.

Too soon, she ended the kiss, gazing up at him with almost...reverence in her eyes. "I'll see you tomorrow."

"Tomorrow." He cleared the hoarseness from his voice and stepped away, rubbing the back of his neck, trying to cool himself down.

"Are you sure you don't want to come in?"

"Yes." He spoke too quickly, earning a little giggle.

Oh, she shouldn't giggle like that. This was hard enough already.

He looked up at the building. No way he should walk her to her door, but he didn't want to leave until he knew she was safe, either. "Is your apartment in the front?"

"Yeah."

"Which one?"

"Third floor." She pointed at a bay window.

"When you're inside, safe and sound with the door locked behind you, wave to me, okay?"

She stepped forward and rested her hand on his chest. "Why don't you just walk me up?"

"You know why."

"Cheesecake?"

"Yeah." His lips tipped up in a smile. "Cheesecake."

She lingered there a long moment. Then she climbed the steps and went inside.

A minute later, she appeared in the bay window and waved.

Mark lifted his hand, then settled in his car, satisfied that she was safe, and cursed himself for a fool.

He'd done the one thing he'd sworn he'd never do. He'd fallen in love.

As much as he wanted to be angry with himself, he knew he was smiling as he drove away.

## CHAPTER FIFTEEN

Amanda continued watching the street even after
Mark's car disappeared around the corner. Maybe he'd
change his mind and come back for dessert—the fattening
kind, anyway.

She hadn't been interested in any men on campus. They
drank too much and talked too loudly. They were arrogant
and irritating, and she didn't trust them.

But Mark was different. Everything about him was different. He was a man of honor, more concerned about her virtue
than his pleasure.

She missed him already.

But he wasn't coming back, not tonight. Reluctantly, she
dropped the curtain and grabbed her phone from her purse.
She left the pepper spray and keychain alarm where they
were and headed for the bedroom, where she plugged her
phone into the charger on her nightstand. She was halfway
through brushing her teeth when her phone rang.

She smiled into the mirror. It was Mark. It had to be.

The phone had stopped ringing by the time she finished,

but she'd call him right back. She was in the hallway when she heard a knock at the door.

She smiled so wide that her cheeks hurt.

He'd returned after all.

She ran to the door and flung it open.

A man stood there, his black hoodie covering shocking white-blond hair, his left eye blackened and swollen.

Gasping, Amanda slammed the door, but he blocked it and stepped in. He grabbed the back of her head with his left hand, covered her mouth with his right, and shoved her inside.

She was off balance, trying to push him away. But she was no match for him.

He swept her feet out from under her, releasing his hold on her head at the same time.

Her back slammed against the hardwood floor. Her breath whooshed out.

She struggled to pull in air, desperate to stand. To run. To scream.

She couldn't. She couldn't do anything.

Ignoring the stabbing pain in her back, she crawled toward the kitchen. Scream! But only the tiniest, raspy noise came out.

She looked over her shoulder.

The man calmly locked the door, then crouched beside her and pushed her onto her side. She pulled her knees up, ducking her head. Still struggling to pull breath into her lungs.

"It was only a matter of time before he left you alone," the intruder said. "Fortunately, I'm a very patient man."

# CHAPTER SIXTEEN

Mark waited for the light to change, tapping his fingers to the beat of the music playing on his stereo. Trying not to think about Amanda.

But she was all he could think about, all he'd thought about since he'd first seen her Thursday night. And now he'd left her alone. Probably with another man.

He figured Carl had wasted no time checking to make sure she was all right. Mark had seen the guy standing in the same spot as he had that morning, a dark shadow in the alley beside Amanda's building. Had he waited there all day?

Obviously, Carl was more into Amanda than she realized. Because to stand there, waiting for her to get home...?

That was stalker behavior.

Mark's neck prickled.

Stalker behavior?

What if the dark figure hadn't been Carl?

What if you're wrong?

The light turned green, but Mark didn't move.

The driver in the car behind him beeped, impatient, but he ignored him.

When the left lane was clear, he yanked the wheel into an illegal U-turn, grabbed his phone and dialed her number.

No answer.

His heart raced as he sped past a bus, through a yellow light, and onto her street. He stopped in the space in front of the hydrant, tires squealing as he hit the brakes.

He lurched from the car, up the stairs, and into the breezeway. The inner door was locked. He pressed every button on the wall.

*Come on, come on.*

Somebody would buzz him through.

A female voice came over the intercom. Not Amanda. "Who is it?"

He took a chance and said, "It's me."

The door buzzed.

So much for security.

He yanked the door and took the stairs two at a time until he reached the third-floor landing. He found the door that must be hers and rapped on it with his fist.

"Amanda?"

He turned the knob. Also locked.

He banged again, louder this time. "Amanda? Are you okay?"

Something smashed.

There was a muffled scream.

Mark kicked the door.

The jamb splintered. The door crashed open.

Inside, a man was scrambling to his feet.

Amanda lay beneath him, a broken lamp scattered in jagged pieces all over the floor.

Mark grabbed the guy's sweatshirt and yanked him away from her.

Amanda scooted back.

Mark smashed the rat's face against the hardwood floor, then punched him in the kidneys, twice.

The stalker curled in a ball.

To be on the safe side, Mark punched him on the side of his head until he slumped. "If you move"— Mark spoke in his ear—"I'll kill you." For good measure, he punched him again.

Keeping his hands on the rat's neck, he looked at Amanda. "Are you all right?"

She nodded. Then shook her head. Her eyes were wide, her gaze jumping from Mark to the figure on the floor.

"You're safe." He scooted to where she leaned against the back of the sofa, pulled off his jacket, and draped it over her. "You're in shock. Can you tell me what hurts?"

She blinked, shook her head again.

"Okay. It's okay." He tucked her against his chest and rubbed her back. "You're safe now."

She didn't speak, though he could feel her trembling.

Two men appeared in the doorway, young enough to be college students. Both wore jeans. One wore a gray sweatshirt, the other a dark blue Johnson & Wales T-shirt. The one in the sweatshirt said, "What happened? Amanda?"

She didn't even look up.

Mark said, "Call 911."

"Right." The T-shirt guy pulled his cell from his pocket and dialed, retreating into the hallway.

Mark spoke to the guy in the sweatshirt. "Get her a blanket, would you?"

"Uh..."

"Try the bedroom."

"Right." He disappeared and, a moment later, reappeared with an afghan, the kind someone's grandmother would knit. "Is this okay?"

"It works." The kid draped it over her, then stood back, eyeing the figure on the floor warily.

Mark backed up to see Amanda's face. "Honey, can you tell me what—?"

The figure on the floor lunged for the door.

Sweatshirt guy shifted out of the way.

Mark disengaged from Amanda and tackled the stalker, landing squarely on his back, then slammed his face into the hardwood floor again. "Do you want me to kill you? Because if you move again, I will beat the last breath out of you." He slammed his head into the floor again. "Do you hear me?"

"Uh-huh." The sound was wet and gurgled.

Mark flipped him over, lifted his head in both his hands, and smashed it into the floor one more time. The man went limp.

Mark looked up to see the T-shirt guy back in the door, eyes wide.

Sweatshirt guy stood in the kitchen with his hands up as if Mark might attack him next.

Amanda sat on the floor. All three of them were staring at him.

"He's alive," Mark said. "If he moves again..."

Sweatshirt guy joined his friend in the doorway. "We won't let him out."

Not that he'd be able to walk a straight line, but Mark nodded his thanks anyway, then asked, "The police?"

"On their way."

"Okay. Thanks." He lifted Amanda off the floor—she weighed less than his pack—and laid her on the sofa. "Tell me what hurts."

Tears filled her eyes. "My back. Everything. But I don't think anything's broken."

Her left cheek was red and swollen. He dabbed it with his fingertip. "He hit you here. Anything else?"

"I'm okay." She rested her head on his chest. "I'm okay, Mark. Thanks to you."

# CHAPTER SEVENTEEN

Amanda blinked her eyes open. It was too bright.

She squinted and stretched and winced at the stabbing pain in her back.

The events of the night before rushed in. She sat up, careful not to move too quickly.

The pain was manageable.

She was on the couch.

Mark was asleep on her old club chair, his head tilted at a terrible angle. The remote control rested on his right knee.

For a few hours, people had packed her apartment. Neighbors and cops, paramedics and firemen.

The police took their statements. While one team of paramedics carried that horrible man away on a gurney, others checked her over thoroughly. They wanted to take her in for X-rays, but the pain in her back had already begun to subside. She had a terrible bruise, but nothing worse.

While she'd been arguing with the EMTs, Mark had located the building manager and asked him to fix the broken door. The man promised to have it fixed the next day, but

Mark wasn't willing to wait. Apparently, he was persuasive, because the manager—usually notoriously slow—pulled a door jamb off an empty apartment and repaired her door right away.

Meanwhile, a couple of her neighbors donned gloves, mopped up the intruder's blood, and swept away the remains of her lamp.

At some point, Mark had searched her kitchen cabinets until he found a small bottle of brandy. She'd bought it to make chocolate mousse for a party, but she'd only used an ounce. After everyone left, Mark poured the rest into two short glasses and handed her one.

"Drink that, please."

"I don't drink."

He traced the bump she could already feel lifting on her cheek. "It's just a tiny bit. It'll help you sleep."

Sleep sounded very good. So she'd sipped the brandy, then swallowed four ibuprofens with a tall glass of water.

She'd showered, scrubbing until her skin was bright red, trying to scour all the remains of that disgusting man off. Then she'd slipped into her pajamas and returned to the couch, where she laid her head on Mark's lap. She couldn't bear to be alone. He stroked her hair with his left hand, sipped what was left of his brandy with his right, and watched sports news.

And like he promised, the brandy went to work, and she drifted off.

It hadn't been a sound sleep. But whenever she woke, Mark was there, whispering in her ear and promising her she was safe.

Because of him, she felt safe and always went right back to sleep.

Mark had still been awake at four, watching the same ESPN broadcast that had been on earlier. One glance at his face told her he wasn't paying any attention to the TV. His mind was elsewhere.

Apparently, he'd finally succumbed to sleep.

Now, it was almost nine o'clock. She tiptoed into the bathroom, then dressed carefully in a roomy sweater that didn't hurt too much when she slipped it over her head. With her cell phone in her back pocket, some cash in her front, and her keys, she steeled her courage and left the apartment silently.

She'd never been afraid to leave her house before, and she wasn't going to start now.

Outside, she squinted in the sun's reflection off the windows across the street. Hugging herself, she turned toward Weybosset. It was Sunday, and the city was quiet. A few cars drove by, trailing white exhaust in the frosty morning air. A jogger approached her, steam rising off his bare shoulders. She stiffened, fearful, but forced herself to continue past him. He barely acknowledged her.

She made it the half-block to the little store on the corner. Inside, she paused to breathe. You're okay. Knock it off. You're okay.

She had eggs and bread at home, so she purchased bacon, an onion, a can of mushrooms, and a couple of potatoes. With those in hand, she headed for the Dunkin' Donuts a couple of blocks down and bought two large coffees before heading back to her apartment.

She felt strong and brave.

But when she peeked into her living room, Mark was gone.

She stared at the empty space.

Had he been waiting for the perfect opportunity to make his getaway?

Had he spent the entire night counting the hours until he could leave her?

After last night, she'd thought maybe he'd make time for breakfast, if nothing else. After all they'd been through, he could've at least said goodbye.

Calling herself all kinds of idiot, she set her purchases on the counter, wincing at the stabbing pain in her back. She filled a glass with tap water and swallowed four more ibuprofens.

At the squeaky sound of the shower faucet and water pouring into the tub, she nearly giggled.

Of course he hadn't left.

She sliced the potatoes into small chunks while vegetable oil heated on the stovetop. She'd almost finished when her phone rang.

"Good morning, sweetheart," her mother said. "Dad and I thought we'd try to catch you before church. How was your week?"

She collapsed into a chair at the kitchen table and told her parents everything.

# CHAPTER EIGHTEEN

After Mark heard Amanda return from wherever she'd gone, he stepped into the shower, letting the hot water massage the tight muscles in his neck and back. Nothing like sleeping in a chair to teach you to appreciate a soft mattress.

He figured he'd be sleeping in a lot worse places than a chair soon enough.

When Amanda had left earlier, he'd barely kept himself from following her. It was healthy for her to go out alone, and it definitely would not be healthy for him to stalk her like that little rat from the night before.

The detective had assured them that the stalker would be in jail at least until his arraignment on Monday.

He'd better stay in jail a lot longer than that.

Mark's cell phone rang. Whoever it was could wait five minutes until he'd finished getting cleaned up.

He used a squirt of liquid soap that filled the tiny shower with the scent of flowers, bringing Amanda to mind.

Not that he minded that, but he wasn't thrilled about smelling like a girl for the rest of the day.

His phone rang again when he was rinsing shampoo out of his hair.

While he dried himself with a towel he'd found in the hall closet, his phone rang a third time. Wrapping the towel around his waist, he looked at the caller ID.

Uh-oh. He connected the call. "Lieutenant Johnson."

"It's Major Sapp. I just got off the phone with Detective Sealy of the Providence PD. You know him?"

"Yes, sir."

"You were involved in an altercation in which you...let me see here..."

Papers were shuffled in the background.

"You repeatedly smashed the head of one Russell T. Harris into a hardwood floor, broke his nose, and gave him a concussion."

Mark felt his future slipping away. "Yes, sir."

More paper shuffling. "You punched him so hard in the kidneys that he's being treated for blood in his urine."

Mark gazed through the haze of steam at the mirror over the sink, seeing only a hazy reflection. "I punched him, sir. I wasn't aware of that."

"Sealy also said that Mr. Harris broke into the apartment of a girl you've been seeing and"—was his CO shuffling the papers to make Mark sweat? If so, it was working—"attempted to sexually assault her."

Mark swallowed. "That's what it looked like, sir."

"I see." Major Sapp was silent for a moment.

His CO was fair. He'd lectured them often about how everyone deserved respect. Fellow soldiers, subordinates, superiors, citizens of enemy nations, enemies, and women. Especially women. Maybe that would help Mark's cause.

Finally, the major spoke again. "I have one question for you, Lieutenant."

"Yes, sir."

"Did it really take you that many hits to knock the guy out?"

Mark blinked. "I was trying not to kill him, sir."

Major Sapp chuckled. "I'm glad you didn't kill him. The paperwork would have been a bear."

Mark blew out a breath and wiped sweat off his brow with the back of his hand. "Yes, sir."

"How's the girl?"

"She'll be all right, as long as... What did you say his name was?"

"Russell T. Harris."

"As long as Harris doesn't get out of jail, Amanda will be okay."

"So, Amanda." Major Sapp paused as if waiting for something, but Mark wasn't sure what. After a minute, the major asked, "Girlfriend?"

"I met her Thursday night. I saw Harris follow her out of the bar where she worked. I...distracted him."

"I see."

"She and I spent some time together this weekend." Such a bland way to describe what had happened over the last twenty-four hours. They'd fallen for each other. They'd fallen in love.

"I don't know how you feel about her," Major Sapp said, "but women don't forget men who save their lives."

"I don't know that I saved her life."

"You did." The amusement drained from the major's voice. "Sealy told me they ran Harris's prints and got a hit.

Two, actually. They pulled a thumbprint off the belt buckle of a college student who was raped, murdered, and left in a dumpster in Albany. There was another match from a crime scene in western Mass."

Mark sat on the side of the tub. It'd be a bad idea to hang up on his superior so he could vomit. "I see."

"I imagine the detective will call soon."

"My phone rang twice before you called."

"He's going to ask you to go to the DA's office tomorrow to sign a statement so you won't have to appear at a trial. I assume that won't be a problem?"

"No, sir." He'd need to stay in Providence another day, which would irritate his mother, but what else was new?

"They're not going to release the guy, right?"

"He won't be granted bail. The only question right now is where he'll stand trial first. Probably New York or Massachusetts, since those would both be murder charges."

At least Amanda wouldn't have to worry about him coming after her again. "Thank God."

"That's right, son. Thank God. Listen, get this taken care of. We expect you with us one week from tomorrow."

"Thank you, sir."

Mark ended the call and stared at the hazy mirror.

He'd saved her life.

Maybe he should've killed the guy.

He slipped into his dirty jeans, wiped the mirror with his towel, and checked his reflection. Not a hair out of place—the good thing about a crew cut.

He opened the bathroom door to let in some cool air. Standing in the hallway, he picked up the unmistakable scent of frying bacon.

"Good morning."

Mark turned to see Amanda behind him wearing jeans, a sweater, and sneakers. Her hair was brushed, her face scrubbed clean of makeup. Despite the bruise on her cheek, she was beautiful. And staring at his bare chest.

"Sorry. It's hot in there."

She looked up and blushed. "The fan's broken. I'm making breakfast."

"Where'd you go?"

"I needed a couple of things. I got you a coffee."

"Thanks. Let me just—"

"Take your time."

Mark slipped back into the bathroom, threw on his sweater, and headed for the kitchen in his bare feet. He leaned on the kitchen counter and watched her from behind as she stirred something in a cast-iron skillet.

"Smells delicious."

She started at his words, and he cursed himself for startling her. She spoke before he could apologize. "It'll be another few minutes." When she turned to him, her face was pale. She nodded to a Dunkin' Donuts cup. "That one's yours."

He reached for it and took a sip. "Perfect. Thanks."

"I just talked to Detective Sealy."

He set the drink down and stepped toward her. "You heard, then?"

"How did you?"

"My CO called."

"Oh." She snatched a paper towel from a roll on the counter and wiped her eyes "They were both killed in alleys.

That would've been me, Thursday. They were both blond-haired and blue-eyed, just like me."

"I didn't hear that part."

"The detective says the guy doesn't stand a chance at getting bail. I guess the only question is, who gets to prosecute him first?"

"Do you care?"

"No. As long as he goes to jail forever."

Mark pulled her into a hug. "I was impressed with you this morning, venturing out by yourself."

She leaned back to meet his eyes. "I knew I was safe. I can't let this derail my whole life, right?"

"Still, it was very brave."

They looked at each other a moment longer, nothing but the crackle of bacon filling the silence.

She turned back to the stove. "I'd better..."

He got out of her way, and she stirred the potatoes, flipped the bacon, then whisked some eggs. "Do you like mushrooms?"

"Sure."

She poured the eggs into a big pan, then lifted each piece of bacon onto a paper towel-covered plate. She set the plate in front of him, so he snagged a piece and took a bite.

Salty and perfectly crisped. "Delicious."

"Thanks." She tended the eggs. "Sealy wants you to call him."

"I will, in a bit." He took another bite.

She twisted toward him. "And my parents want to talk to you."

He almost choked on his bacon, gulped the coffee, scalding his tongue. "Your parents? Why?"

Her eyebrows lifted, amusement playing around her mouth. "I told them what happened. I guess they want to thank you."

"Oh. Okay." What in the world would he say? Wasn't it too soon to meet the parents?

He stood, needed to do something and feeling like a fool for being so nervous. "Can I set the table?"

"Help yourself."

He found the plates and silverware, then added salt, pepper, and a jar of salsa from the fridge.

While Mark ate his breakfast—an omelet, fried potatoes, bacon, and toast, and if he hadn't already fallen for her, the meal would have pushed him over the edge—Amanda moved food around on her plate. For someone who wanted to be a chef, she sure didn't eat much.

But she did make small talk, and he loved listening to her, the lilt of her voice, the Massachusetts accent he guessed had been softened by summers in Florida the last few years with her parents. She talked about their house, which was within walking distance of Satellite Beach, and her brothers and their wives, who'd all moved south as well. She talked about how her parents were always talking up the wonders of their new home state.

"I know they want me to move there, but I'm not going to. I like it here."

"They'll probably understand." His father would, and her parents sounded like reasonable people. He added, "I don't need their thanks." Maybe he could get out of calling them.

"Oh." Her expression dimmed. "They want to meet you."

He didn't want to disappoint Amanda. Or them.

At least they didn't live next door. A phone call, he could handle.

After finishing both their breakfasts, he grabbed her plate. "You cooked, so I'll clean."

She took it back and set it on the counter. Then she grabbed her phone. "I'll clean, and you talk to my parents."

He stifled a groan while she dialed. "Mom? You still want to talk to Mark?" Amanda grinned at him, then said, "Okay. Here he is," and held out the phone.

He stood tall, as if he were lining up for inspection. "Hello."

"This is Amanda's mom, Lydia."

"Lieutenant Mark Johnson, United States Marine Corps." He sounded so formal. What an idiot.

"This is her dad, Paul."

"We can't thank you enough for saving our baby." Lydia had tears in her voice. Like mother, like daughter. "We needed to tell you how much we appreciate what you did. You can't imagine..." Her words were choked off by a sob.

Paul picked up the thread. "Not a lot of men would've gone to the lengths you did to keep her safe."

"It wasn't that much," he said.

"It was. It was all that and more." Lydia's voice was stronger. "Who knows what would've happened if not for you?"

Mark knew, but he wasn't about to tell Amanda's parents the news about her attacker. Amanda was watching from across the kitchen. She lifted her eyebrows, and he shrugged.

Paul cleared his throat. "She said you spent the night."

"On the couch. I mean, she slept on the couch, sir, and I slept on the chair. She didn't want to be alone."

"So she said." Paul didn't sound upset, just matter-of-fact.

"Nothing happened, obviously—"

"Thank you for that too. A lot of men would've taken advantage of the situation."

"No, sir. Of course not."

Lydia said, "Mark, Mandy tells us you're being sent to Afghanistan."

Mandy. He liked that nickname. "I leave a week from tomorrow."

"That's horrible business over there," Lydia said. "I'm sorry you have to go." She paused, but what was he supposed to say? That he was sorry to be going off to war? He wasn't sorry.

But across the room, Amanda was washing dishes, sending him glances every few seconds, and a stab of regret pierced him. If not for the Marines and terrorists and Afghanistan, he could stay here, with her.

Maybe he wasn't so happy after all.

He must've paused too long because Lydia spoke again. "I hope you don't mind if Mandy gives us your contact information. We'd like to send you care packages now and then. Would that be okay?"

They wanted to send him care packages? His own mother wouldn't do that.

Before he recovered from his surprise, Paul said, "Uh, Lydia, could I talk to Mark for a second? Alone?"

"Oh. Okay. It was good to talk to you. I'll pray for you every day."

"Thank you, ma'am. I appreciate that."

She hung up, and Amanda's father cleared his throat.

"Listen, son. It's not that I don't appreciate what you did for my daughter. I do."

Uh-oh.

This couldn't be good.

"But you're obviously quite older than she is."

"Six years." He refrained from adding the *only*, though it was on the tip of his tongue.

"It's not just the years," Paul said. "You're a soldier, about to go off to war."

A Marine, not a soldier, but he didn't correct him as he wandered down the hallway and stepped into the bathroom, closing the door behind him. Whatever her father wanted to say, Mark had a feeling he might need some privacy.

"My brother went to Vietnam," Paul continued, "and it changed him. You might not come home the same."

Mark heard what the man wasn't saying.

*You might not come home at all.*

"I'm sure you're a good guy, but she's my daughter, and I'm only trying to protect her. I'm just saying, maybe you shouldn't make her any promises. Just keep it casual until you get home. Encourage her to see other people, and you do the same, and then, when you get out, if you both still feel the same way—"

"You're right." The words twisted his insides, but he forced himself to add, "Of course you're right. I told her the same thing last night, but she can be persuasive, and... Well, she's amazing, so I let her..." He took a breath.

He didn't want to end things with Amanda.

But he needed to.

He'd decided a long time ago that he didn't want to get married. He didn't want to commit himself to a woman. His dad had stuck it out with his mother throughout their long, terrible marriage, when Mark would've bailed years before. He'd told his father as much, more than once.

The Marines wouldn't have to change him. Battle wouldn't have to change him. Mark already didn't want what Amanda would expect from him. Mark already knew he wasn't the man for her or any woman. And he didn't want to be.

No matter what he felt for her, this weekend had been a fantasy.

One Amanda's father had seen right through.

"I'll end it today."

"I'm not saying—"

"Don't worry." Mark swallowed all his feelings. "This has nothing to do with you. She needs someone who can be with her now, not some Marine half a world away." Not a guy who, even if he kept himself from getting blown up in Afghanistan, would bail at the first sign of trouble.

AMANDA HAD BEEN TEMPTED to listen through the door at Mark's end of the conversation. What was he hiding from her? Didn't he know her parents would tell her everything?

Knowing that, she hadn't bothered. She was elbow-deep in dishes when Mark walked in. "I need to go. I have to call my parents and let them know I won't be home today. And make sure it's okay with Justin if I stay until tomorrow."

Her heart did a backflip. "You're staying?"

"I have to give my statement tomorrow."

"Should we do something, or—?"

"I'm sorry." He set her phone on the counter. "This thing between you and me... It's not going to work."

"What?" She must have misheard him. But her heart thumped, and her pulse raced, and her voice was barely a whisper. "I don't understand. What...what are you saying?"

"You won't be hearing from me again."

"Did my parents—?"

"This has nothing to do with them. I don't like commitment."

"You're committed to the Marines."

He crossed his arms. "Let me rephrase. I don't want you waiting for me. I won't wait for you."

She felt the sting of tears behind her eyes and blinked them back. He wasn't telling her the truth. He was trying to get her to move on. She had to believe that. "You can't keep me from waiting for you. And when you get back—"

"If I get back—"

"Don't say that!"

"Why not? It's true. I'll be in combat. I could be injured or killed. No matter what happens, I won't come back the person I am right now."

"You'll be better."

"I wouldn't count on it." He moved into her small living area and sat to put on his shoes.

Amanda perched on the arm of the couch, preparing her argument.

But when he looked at her, his features had hardened into a cold, emotionless mask, and her words died on her lips.

"It's not what I want." He closed his mouth in a tight line and looked down to tie his sneakers. "I have no intention of marrying, ever. It's not just that I'm going to war—that's my excuse today. When I get home, there'll be another one." He plopped his foot on the floor and stood, glaring down at her. "I don't want to get married, not to you or anyone else."

Amanda looked away, not able to bear the fury in his eyes.

"Who said anything about marriage?"

He blew out a breath. "Talking to your parents... They're great, but obviously, that's what they want for you. And what you want. It's what you deserve."

At his softening tone, she risked turning toward him again.

"If I were to change my mind, you'd definitely be..." He faltered, looked at the floor. "I don't want to lead you on, that's all."

"How kind of you to think of that now." She infused her tone with sarcasm. It was either that or give in to the heartache trying to work its way up her throat. "I suppose I should thank you for not waiting a year or two before you dumped me. Or sleeping with me first."

Had she imagined his feelings? Had she led herself to believe that a man who'd gone to such lengths to save her life must, by extension, love her?

Or that he must love her because she loved him?

"I'd better go."

"I guess so."

"I'm sorry."

"You don't owe me anything."

He walked to the door and grabbed the knob. He didn't turn around when he spoke. "Tell the building manager to reinforce the deadbolt. It shouldn't be so easy to kick in."

What do you care? That was what she wanted to say. "Okay."

And he was gone.

# CHAPTER TWENTY

Mark's car still smelled faintly of Amanda. He breathed deeply, then rolled down the windows, letting in the chilly November air. He had to get the thought of her out of his head. She represented everything he didn't want for his life.

He'd been honest with her, after all. He'd never planned to get married or commit himself to any woman.

His emotions had gotten the better of him, and he'd let himself believe he could have something out of his reach.

But a happy marriage wasn't in the cards for Mark. His father swore Mom had been sweet and lovely back when they'd first married, but she'd turned on him years before.

Dad was ten times the man Mark would ever be, and he was miserable. If Dad couldn't make marriage work, there was no way Mark could.

He loved his mother because she'd given birth to him—apparently after forty hours of hard labor, though the number changed depending on how angry she was. Thanks to that terrible labor, she hadn't been able to have other children, though Mark suspected she hadn't wanted any more.

He loved her in that you're-my-mother-and-I-have-to way. But if he had half a brain, he'd quit calling her and just communicate with his dad.

But that was Mark's problem. He was loyal too. He knew, deep down, that if he were married to a woman like Mom, he'd stay with her and live a miserable life. Rather than divorce, he'd just beg for a premature death.

Why would any man agree to that?

Why would he sign up to watch Amanda turn from the sweet, innocent beauty she was today into a hateful, bitter shrew?

He'd rather be alone, thank you very much.

Now that he was away from her and those big, blue eyes, he felt sane again.

The hollow feeling in his gut would go away. He'd forget about Amanda. He had to.

He parked on the street near Justin's condo. At the door, he knocked, then let himself in.

Justin was sitting at the kitchen table dressed in gray sweatpants and a Black Dog T-shirt, a cup of coffee in his hand. He peered over his newspaper, eyebrows waggling. "Quite a lunch date."

Mark plopped on the couch. "It wasn't like that."

"Really?"

"She's not that kind of girl."

Justin laughed, full and hearty, as if he hadn't heard anything so funny in months. "Where'd you take her, the fifties?"

A chop to his throat would shut him up. A punch to the solar plexus, maybe. Instead, Mark went into the kitchen and grabbed a coffee mug.

Justin followed and stopped at the edge of the small kitchen. "Just a joke, man. What's your problem?"

Mark poured some coffee, took a sip, and set it down. "I slept in a chair."

Justin chuckled, but at Mark's glare, the sound died. "Did something happen?"

Mark skimmed over the events of the day but told him all about the attack the night before. When he finished, he fell onto the couch.

Justin followed and plopped in his chair. "Wow. He's a serial killer?"

"Yup."

"So, was it that server with all the metal on her face?"

"The other one. The blonde. Amanda."

"She's..." Justin paused.

Mark met his eyes, waiting for him to churn out one of his typical Justin compliments. The degrading kind. Justin swallowed and said, "Pretty."

They sat in silence.

Mark still needed to call his mom and tell her he wouldn't be home. He wasn't looking forward to that conversation. He needed to call the detective. Hopefully, he'd be able to set up the interview for early the following day. The sooner he got out of Providence, the better.

Other than those two calls, he had nothing to do but wait for the day to be over.

He hadn't even asked Amanda about her bruises. Did she feel okay? Was she hurting? Was she nervous, all by herself?

Was she thinking of him?

He stood, looked around.

"Where you going?" Justin asked.

He sat again. "I don't know."

His friend stared at him, eyes narrowed. "I don't understand something."

"What?"

"Why are you here? I mean, after everything you did for this woman, all the time you spent with her, you obviously have feelings for her."

"We just met."

"So what? Everybody meets their somebody at some point. Maybe you just met, but that doesn't mean—"

"Let it go." Mark was too tired, his emotions too close to the surface, to have this conversation again. "I'm deploying."

"Not to be repetitive, but so what?"

"I'm not getting married."

"Grow up, man." Justin pushed to his feet. "We're not children anymore."

"What's that supposed to mean?"

"You know what it means." His friend returned to the kitchen table, grabbed his coffee cup, and dumped the remains in the sink.

Mark did know.

They'd been eleven years old, and Mark's parents had just had another one of their episodes. Not fights. They never fought in front of him. Instead, his mother would make some cutting remark, his father would give her his signature look and walk away. That look said so many things. Mostly it said, Will I ever be good enough for you? A question Mark had asked himself a million times.

This time, Justin had seen everything. They'd decided marriage wasn't worth the hassle.

Justin washed his cup, then grabbed the coffee carafe. "Do you know why I asked Marie to marry me?"

"She wore you down?"

"I broke our pact because I met the right woman."

"I'm happy for you."

"But you'll never do it."

"I won't."

Justin dumped the coffee grinds into the trash, then leaned on the counter toward Mark, his hands clasped together. "Not every woman is like your mother."

"I'd watch my mouth, if I were you." It was one thing for Mark to talk about her, but...

"I know, I know." He pushed himself up. "You can probably kill me without getting off the couch."

Mark didn't bother to respond.

"But as your oldest friend, I have to say this." Justin returned to the living room and sat in the chair opposite him. "Your mother..."

Mark lifted one eyebrow.

"She isn't what I would call a warm woman."

Mark resisted the urge to smile. His mother was warm like Hitler.

Justin's Adam's apple bobbed. "She's..."

"What?" Never satisfied? Never happy? Never forgotten a mistake? Never noticed an accomplishment?

"Not every woman is your mother."

Mark rubbed the back of his neck. "I heard once that men tend to marry women like their mothers. I'd rather be alone than be saddled with..." He wasn't going to finish that. "Why am I talking to you about this? I should pummel you."

"You're talking to me because I know how she treated

you. I know how she treats your father. Maybe if she were my mother, I wouldn't want to get married, either."

"Not everybody had Donna Reed for a mother."

"You had Mommy Dearest."

Mark stood. "Seriously. Shut up."

"There are a lot of good women out there."

Mark was leaving. And her father didn't want him making her promises. And...and he'd made a stupid pact when he was eleven.

No. He wasn't changing his mind. He'd be better off without her. And she'd be better off without him. End of story. "It doesn't matter."

"I'm guessing it matters to her."

"She's barely old enough to drink. How can she understand what it would be like to be stuck with a Marine? With a veteran, assuming I make it home."

"So you dumped her for her own good."

"You can't dump someone you're not with. We just met."

"And you don't have any feelings for her?"

Mark didn't answer that. He didn't want to lie.

"Of course you don't." Justin reclined in the chair. "She's just some brainless bimbo."

The words weren't out of his mouth before Mark grabbed him by the front of his shirt and yanked him to his feet.

His friend smiled. "Yeah, it's really obvious you don't care about her."

"Shut up." He pushed him back into the chair and walked out.

# CHAPTER TWENTY-ONE

Amanda stepped out of the red brick building, stopping to zip up her jacket and tug on her gloves. It was a cold, overcast day.

She wished she'd asked a friend to come to the police station with her, but anyone she'd asked would've had to miss class to join her. Anyway, it was Mark's company she craved, and he was long gone.

She'd spent almost an hour with a detective, a prosecutor, and an FBI agent, going over everything that'd happened Saturday night, then going back to Thursday night at the bar and on her way home.

When she finally finished answering all their questions, she learned they'd turned up a fourth victim—another young woman found dead on a college campus. So far, Amanda was the only one to have survived.

She shuddered, not wanting to consider what might have happened as she turned toward her apartment.

And froze.

Mark was standing on the sidewalk, facing her. He

looked dashing in his uniform—khaki colored with a matching hat and a light brown shirt and tie.

Amanda's heart fluttered, and she hurried toward him. He was so handsome in that uniform—so much better than Superman. How had someone she'd known only a few days become so important to her?

He was waiting for her. Her heart soared. Of course he hadn't meant what he'd said the morning before.

"I saw you go in."

There was something in his posture and his tone that had her stopping a few feet away from him.

"I needed to grab some lunch," Mark continued, "and I wanted to make sure you're okay."

"Oh."

"Are you? Okay?"

She didn't know how to answer that question.

He approached her slowly. When he got close enough, he lifted his hand and traced his finger along the bruise beneath her eye.

It looked worse today, black and puffy. No makeup had covered it.

He swallowed, closed his mouth in a line, and shifted his hand to her hair. He slid his fingers down a lock, and her whole body tingled.

She jerked away.

"Sorry."

Sorry? He was sorry? For what? For touching her? For leaving her? Or waiting for her? For breaking her heart?

For saving her life?

What was she supposed to say in response to *sorry*?

"How are you?" His voice was warm, his tone tender.

She stiffened, mustering anger to keep her tears at bay. "What difference does it make?"

"I care, Amanda. I just—"

"Just not that much. I get it." She started walking.

He fell into step beside her. "Mind if I walk you home?"

"Why?"

"Because... I thought you might be nervous."

"He was denied bail."

"I know. Still." He matched her pace.

"I walk around this city by myself all the time." She glared at him. "I don't need you to protect me."

He flinched as if she'd wounded him, and regret poured over her.

"I'm sorry." Stupid tears. She swiped them away, walking a few steps until she thought her voice would sound normal. "You don't owe me anything."

"You don't owe *me* anything."

Great. They were even-steven. Just what she wanted.

He shook his head, a little smile on his lips. "After what happened Saturday, I thought you'd be nervous to walk by yourself. You're very brave."

"He's being extradited to New York."

"Fear isn't always rational."

Mark would know. Whatever fear had him running away from her certainly wasn't.

At the corner, Amanda turned toward her apartment and campus.

When Mark took her hand, her breath caught. It felt so right, being with him. Obviously to him too. Did he even realize what he'd done?

Maybe she should yank her hand back, but she couldn't

do it. She couldn't make herself put distance between them. If that was what Mark wanted, he was going to have to do it.

They walked in silence, her thoughts swirling like leaves in the wind. She told herself to keep quiet and enjoy the moment, but words escaped against her will. "We're not even going to talk about this?"

He squeezed her hand, and she wished she'd skipped the gloves. She wanted to feel the warmth of his skin against hers.

"About what?"

"About you and me."

His lips pressed in that tight line that told her he wasn't happy. "There is no you and me, Amanda. I'm going to be gone for a long time. I'm sorry that you think there's some future for us, but there isn't."

"You'll be home, eventually."

"Hopefully."

"Don't say—"

"By then, you'll have met somebody else, somebody more appropriate."

Stopping, she tugged her hand from his and faced him. "You're okay with that."

"It's the right thing to do."

"And you'll be seeing other people?"

He smirked. "I'm going to Afghanistan. They wear burkas over there. I won't be seeing any women."

"I'm sure you'll get vacations."

"Leave."

"Plenty of opportunities to date."

He shrugged but said nothing.

Fine, then. "Carl came by yesterday. He asked me out. You don't mind if I go out with him?"

Emotions played across Mark's face. His Adam's apple dipped, but he said, "Nope. I think you should."

She nodded slowly. "If he takes me out Friday night, we'll probably have a few drinks. He likes to drink."

"You don't."

"I can learn. And then when we get home, maybe I'll invite him up for dessert. You're okay with that?"

"You still have that cheesecake—"

"That's not the dessert I mean."

Mark blinked a few times, swallowed again.

"You don't care if I date him? Or another man? If I invite them to my apartment...if I invite them to my bed—?"

"Amanda." He groaned, looking toward the sky. "Please don't."

"I thought you didn't care."

His gaze snapped to her. "I never said that." His eyes blazed with emotion. "What do you want me to say?"

"How about the truth?"

He stepped back and crossed his arms.

"Okay. I'll start." Now or never, because once he walked out of her life, she might never see him again.

Decimated buildings. Suicide bombers. Caskets draped with flags. Images of war flashed through her mind. Anything could happen. He might not come home. And she couldn't live with the idea that he might die without knowing.

He thought she was brave for walking to the police station by herself, but that was nothing compared to telling him how she felt—and how deeply she felt it—knowing he'd probably reject her. But she had to do it. He was worth the risk. "Thursday night, I thought you were following me. Friday, I wasn't sure if you were a superhero or a stalker. But sometime on Saturday, between the fish tacos and the mall, I fell in love with you."

Mark didn't move. He barely breathed.

"And it's not because you saved my life—twice. It's more than that. You're everything I want in a man, everything I ever wanted."

She waited for some response, some reaction. But there was nothing. "Look me in the eye, Mark, and tell me you don't care for me."

Another beat passed, and hope flared inside.

But then, he looked down, leaned in, and kissed her on the cheek. "I'm sorry."

He turned and walked away.

# CHAPTER TWENTY-TWO

As soon as Mark was around the corner, he broke into a run, skirting people and bikes and dogs.

He had to get away from her.

He knew what he wanted for his life. No commitments. No relationships. No woman demanding things from him. He wouldn't give up his plans. Not for Amanda. Not for anyone.

He should be happy he'd avoided that trap.

But all he felt was...sick.

What was he doing?

None of this made sense. Mark had saved a total stranger from an attacker.

No. A rapist.

Not just a rapist. A serial killer.

He'd saved her not because he was amazing but because... because he'd been given good instincts. He was part of a bigger plan.

Which meant there was a Planner.

Which meant Amanda was supposed to be part of Mark's life.

What did that mean?

Mark didn't know enough about God to answer that. He should've actually paid attention in church instead of pretending to in an effort to avoid his mother's wrath.

She was the reason he felt so conflicted.

But Amanda wasn't anything like his mother.

No, Amanda was kind and encouraging and honest. She hadn't asked Mark for anything except that he not discard her. She would be the one to do all the sacrificing if they stayed together. While she'd have plenty of opportunities to date, he'd be stuck in the desert, surrounded by Marines.

What was he running from?

He slowed to a stop.

Was he really willing to let her go because of some misguided fear of women? Would he really let his mother's hate dictate his entire life?

He'd worked so hard to do his own thing, despite his mother and her demands. She'd been furious when he turned down Princeton in favor of the Academy. When it came time for him to choose a branch of the service, she'd insisted he choose the Navy.

He'd bucked his mother's demands in every area of his life, congratulating himself on how he hadn't let her define him or choose his life's goals.

But here he was, letting his fear of ending up with someone like his mother scare him away from the woman he loved.

Beautiful, sweet Amanda was nothing like Patricia Truman Johnson.

Amanda loved him, and her love wasn't demanding or cruel or manipulative. It was true and real. A love he could count on.

A love that would give him hope.

And like a fool, he'd walked away.

He turned and sprinted, dodging pedestrians and dogs, hurrying back to where he'd left Amanda. But she wasn't there.

He continued to her building, pressed the intercom for her apartment.

No answer.

He pressed again and again.

Come on, come on.

She'd answer, wouldn't she?

She would. She would hope it was him. Even now, she believed in him.

She couldn't have gone far. To a friend's maybe?

To Carl's?

Mark would not consider that, not that he'd have anyone to blame but himself.

He jogged to the corner and looked down Weybosset in both directions.

*There.*

She was moving fast, but he was faster.

He hopped off the sidewalk and bolted down the street, ignoring the cars whizzing by and the glares of drivers. When he got close, he slowed to catch his breath, then came up behind her.

"Amanda?"

She spun, startled, eyes wide. Tears dripped down her cheeks and off her chin. Tears he'd put there.

Emotions bubbled up inside him and stole his words. He took her hands and tugged her out of the way of passersby into the entrance of a shop—the bakery, he realized, where he'd watched her with the kids the other day.

Where he'd first started falling for her.

He wrapped his arms around her, trying to think of what to say, how to tell her what he felt. But there were no words.

Her eyes were wide and filled not with fear or anger but hope and the tender love.

He couldn't help himself. He dipped his head and wrapped her up and kissed her. And everything he wanted to say—everything he wanted in life—he poured into that kiss.

When her arms snaked around his neck, when her back arched and she rose on her tiptoes to meet him, he dove in.

Afraid he'd lost her. Then afraid he'd lose her. Afraid he'd mess it up or make her angry or make her hate him or mostly afraid that someday, he'd hate her. And he didn't know what to do with any of those fears. He only knew he loved her. He wanted her and only her.

The truth of it calmed him, and he rested in what he knew to be true. He didn't have the answers, and he didn't need to.

He slowed down. There was no rush. This didn't need to be a kiss that lasted forever but a forever kind of kiss.

Yes, he let it languish, laughing at himself. He'd never put so much thought into a single kiss.

Or into a single woman.

He had a feeling he'd be putting a lot more thought into this one.

Maybe he owed her a few words, though. He forced

himself to stop but didn't let her go. He held her close, feeling her quick breath against his neck.

The world went on around them. People chatted. Cars drove by. Music and the smell of baked goods carried outside through the bakery door whenever it opened.

Mostly, Mark picked up the scent of Amanda's hair and felt her warmth in his arms. "I fell in love with you right here."

She laughed and backed away to look at him. Though there were still tears, they were happy tears now. "When I accused you of stalking me?"

"A few minutes before that. When I was watching you teach the kids."

"So you were stalking me?"

"Not stalking. Observing. Big difference."

She grinned, but it didn't last. "Are you going to change your mind again?"

"No. I'm not. I promise. But it's going to be hard on both of us, me being there, you being here."

"I know."

"I don't think you do."

She took her time before she spoke again. "Okay. I have no idea how it's going to feel, but I'll figure it out. We'll figure it out. And I'll be waiting when you get home."

He liked that, knowing she'd be here. "You should know..." He hadn't thought this part through. "Your father's not excited about us being together. He thinks—"

"Is that why you—?"

"He just said a few things that led me to doubt myself. It was my fears that deceived me."

"I'll talk to him."

"No. I wanted you to know because I don't want secrets between us. But I'll talk to him. Over time, I'll prove myself to him. He'll see."

She regarded him a long moment. "If that's what you want."

"It is. And, if you change your mind about me—"

"Don't." She pressed a finger over his lips. "Don't do that. You've protected me enough. You don't need to protect me from you."

And he didn't need to protect himself from her.

When he returned from Afghanistan—and he'd do everything in his power to ensure he did—he would marry this woman. There was still so much they didn't know about each other. But they would learn together. Grow together.

And stay together. No matter what.

Amanda waited outside the gate area at Logan Airport, clutching a small bouquet of multicolored tulips. Because of the unpredictable Boston traffic, she'd left much earlier than necessary and arrived twenty minutes before. She couldn't wait to see Mark, to feel his arms around her, to feel his breath on her face.

She couldn't wait to feel his lips against hers, to welcome him home with a kiss.

According to the screen overhead, his flight was due any second. Had time ever moved so slowly?

It was Friday afternoon, and people jostled for position all around her. If Mark were returning with his platoon, there would be spouses and children and family and friends, eager to welcome their returning heroes. There'd be signs and flags and balloons, music and fanfare.

Mark deserved all that and more, but he was arriving without his platoon, home for a few weeks to recover from an injury.

"It's minor—nothing to worry about," he'd assured

Amanda on a rare and precious phone call a few days earlier. "The doctors won't clear me for duty for thirty days, and Major Sapp insisted I recuperate stateside."

Insisted?

Amanda hadn't asked why his CO had been forced to insist. Mark had been drowsy and distracted. He hadn't told her about what he'd been through—not on that call or in any of his emails or letters. He hadn't shared details about his injury. He hadn't told her about any of the difficulties he must've faced. Instead, he kept their conversations focused on her and her life. Occasionally, he talked about the future. But when she asked about his world, he kept his remarks surface-level—the weather, his living conditions, his buddies.

Amanda had read everything she could get her hands on about the war in Afghanistan, and though she didn't know exactly what Mark endured, she knew, regardless of what he said about his injury, none of it had been minor.

If Mark was conflicted about returning home, she wouldn't heap guilt on him for it. All she wanted was for him to feel welcome and comfortable and loved.

If only she didn't have to share him with his parents.

The thought of them made her stomach flip, as if she weren't already nervous enough. After she and Mark had spent those amazing—well, bizarre and amazing—days together, he'd been deployed. Since then, they'd shared letters and emails and a couple of phone calls, but this would be the first time she'd seen him since the weekend she'd met him.

The first time in a year and a half.

What if his feelings had changed? What if...?

She shook off her fears. He'd called her, hadn't he? He

wanted her there. And she knew her feelings hadn't changed. With every word he'd written, she'd fallen a little more in love.

Stragglers from the previous flights wandered down the aisle created by retractable belt barriers and toward baggage claim. People surrounded the barrier on both sides, some glancing at watches, others chatting while they waited for arriving passengers.

Two college-aged guys across from Amanda were trying to decide what bar to go to that night. One older woman beside her complained about the increased security since the September eleventh attacks as if they weren't warranted. Funny how quickly people forgot what'd happened.

A loud voice joined the cacophony. "...cannot imagine why he invited that girl." The woman speaking must've stopped a few feet behind Amanda, because by the end of her sentence, her words were clear.

"Because he cares for her." A man answered with a patient tone that implied he'd endured this conversation before. "He wants to see her."

Amanda glanced at the screen, which showed that Mark's plane had just landed.

"He barely knows her." The woman let out an arrogant humph. "He spent two nights with her and fancies himself in love. You'd think a Marine would be a little more worldly."

Amanda stiffened, her nerves zinging with awareness.

Surely...surely these weren't Mark's parents.

When Mark had invited her to meet his plane, he'd warned her that his mother probably wouldn't welcome her. Come to think of it, there'd been no probably about it. "No pressure," he'd said. "I want to see you more than anything, but I can come to Providence after I spend a couple of days with them. You don't need to meet them yet."

Didn't she, though?

She was in love with their son, and he was in love with her. Of course they needed to meet.

Second thoughts...and third and fourth...assailed her now.

But she was jumping to conclusions.

"Give him some credit," the man said. "Mark knows his own mind."

Mark.

Oh, no.

Was it too late to run?

"Pfft. Please." The woman scoffed. "He's been surrounded by sweaty men and burkas for a year and a half. Of course he's eager to see the girl again. If he'd just wait a few days, he could find a willing bedmate—"

"Patricia!" The man's voice was low but vehement. "This is our son you're talking about."

"Don't be such a prude. You know that's all this is. I'm sure she's not as pretty as she is easy."

Indignation had Amanda's heart pounding. She wanted to turn around and give this woman a piece of her mind. But this woman was the mother of the man she loved. Amanda needed to think before she said something she couldn't take back.

She definitely didn't need to be overhearing this conversation. She inched away, but the crowd was as thick and unyielding as over-kneaded dough.

"I will not have you talking about my son that way." Mr.

Johnson's voice hummed with anger. "And you will be kind to Amanda."

If she'd held onto hope that she'd been wrong about who was talking, it vanished there.

Amanda was close enough to hear Mrs. Johnson put-upon sigh. "I suppose it's just for one meal. It won't be long before Mark remembers who he really loves. I don't care who this woman is, she's no Annalise."

*Annalise?*

"You're going to have to let it go." Did the man sound disappointed? "He's made it clear they're not getting back together."

Who was Annalise?

Someone Mark had been with. Someone his parents liked.

Amanda felt sick.

She reached the end of the barrier just as two people hurried through from the gate area. Had they been on Mark's flight?

Amanda's jostling put her in front of a couple of women who'd been there before her.

"Do you mind?" one said.

"Sorry. Let me just..." She scooted to the side, trying to get out of the way.

And then, Mark stepped into view.

She froze, unable to take her eyes off him. Unable to move.

Oh. She'd forgotten. How had she forgotten?

Not just how tall he was, how broad and beautiful. How strong and powerful and fierce.

She'd forgotten the way everything inside her leaned toward him like iron to a magnet.

Behind her, one of the women breathed a low, "Yes, please," earning a giggle from her friend.

Amanda wasn't laughing. This was her Mark, no question, but he was different. He looked older. Tougher. More guarded.

Haunted.

She scanned him, searching for a sign he was in pain. He seemed healthy and whole in his camouflage uniform, his hat tucked under one arm, his duffle bag slung over his other shoulder. He scanned the crowd, skimming right past his parents as if he hadn't noticed them.

His gaze landed on Amanda, and he picked up his pace. He didn't smile, but relief filled in his eyes as if he were dying of thirst and she were a pool of clear water.

Though she itched to launch herself forward, she stayed behind the security line. Had time ever moved so slowly?

"Mark!" His mother had pushed her way to the front and was waving at him. "Mark, sweetie."

He cringed. Visibly cringed.

His expression shifted to apologetic, and disappointment clouded her vision as she watched the man she loved step around the barrier and draw his parents away from the crowd before dropping his bag and greeting them.

Amanda walked toward them but stopped a few feet away.

Mark's dad was about two inches shorter than his son, dark-haired and barrel-chested. He had a wide smile and kind eyes, and Mark resembled him so much that Amanda couldn't help liking the older man immediately. Of course, some of that came from having overheard his remarks earlier.

His mother was tall and slender, her blond hair cut to chin-length, sharp as a cleaver. Her face was thin, her nose and cheekbones so prominent that Amanda could imagine the skull beneath. She had a bright yellow cardigan draped over her shoulders like she'd just stepped off a golf course. Her sleeveless sheath dress showed off ivory arms, long fingers, and sharp claws.

Nails. Not claws.

Even so, as she wrapped her arms around Mark's neck, Amanda had the irrational urge to shout a warning.

Mark survived the dragon's embrace and leaned back to kiss her cheek. They said a few words to each other, and then he stepped away.

When his eyes locked with Amanda's, the force of his gaze had her heart stuttering. Before it regained its rhythm, he was there, sliding his arms around her waist. He pulled her close, lifting her off her feet, holding her against his chest as if she weighed nothing.

"Sweetheart." The word was a warm breath in her ear. "I missed you so much."

Arms around him, she nestled against his shoulder, inhaling his scent, musky and perfect. There was so much she wanted to say, but her throat clogged with tears. She clung to him and cried and hoped this moment would never end.

He didn't rush her, just held her while her breath hitched.

Finally, she managed, "I'm so glad you're home."

"Me too." His voice pitched a little lower. "I'm sorry for what's about to—"

"Well, aren't you going to introduce us?" His mother didn't bother to hide her irritation.

Mark sighed and let Amanda slide to the floor. She caught the barest hint of pain in his expression before he took her hand and faced his parents.

"Mom and Dad, I'd like you to meet Amanda Prince. Amanda, my parents, Hayden and Patricia Johnson."

"Hello, dear." The two words dripped with sarcasm. "How lovely you could be here."

"Nice to meet you, Mrs. Johnson." Amanda lifted her hand to shake, only then remembering the flowers.

Mark quirked an eyebrow. "For me?" By the look on his face, he hoped not.

"Uh, no." She held them to his mom. "For you."

"Tulips." Her lips turned up in a look nobody would mistake for a smile.

"For spring," Amanda said. "Mark told me you're having a party tomorrow, and I thought, for company..."

"Well." She seemed reluctant but took the gift. "They are certainly...pastel."

There was no suitable response to that.

Mark's father stepped into the tense silence. "Call me Hayden. Pleasure to meet you." He shook Amanda's hand, clasping it in both of his. "Mark's told us so much about you. It's wonderful to finally meet you."

"Thank you. I feel the same." About meeting him, anyway.

"You know where we're having lunch?" Mrs. Johnson asked.

"Yes, Mark said—"

"You have a car?"

"I'm parked in—"

"Good. You can meet us there. Mark, as soon as you change out of that getup, we'll leave. Let's go." She spun and stalked away.

Had she just called his uniform a getup? Amanda was still reeling from that remark when Mark leaned in and spoke to his dad, who nodded and followed his wife.

Mark took Amanda's hand. "I'll ride with you."

"I don't think... Don't you need to change?"

He straightened as if she'd wounded him. "Do you want me to change?"

"No. I think you look...beautiful."

His eyebrows hiked, and he almost smiled.

"But your mom—"

The expression faded. "Ignore her. Where are you parked?"

Amanda started toward the door she'd entered, opposite the way his folks had gone, and he hefted his duffle bag and followed.

"She's going to be angry," Amanda said. "She already hates me."

"Right." Mark stopped to face her, and the force of it, the force of him, silenced her. He was there. Right there, after so long.

And, wow, she loved this man.

Which made his mother's reaction so much worse.

Emotion prickled her eyes.

Mark dropped his bag again, seemingly unaware of the

crowd streaming by in both directions. He wiped a tear from her cheek. "It doesn't matter. She doesn't matter."

"It's true?" He hadn't argued, so he must agree. This was a nightmare.

"My mother's opinion is irrelevant, Amanda." He trailed his fingers on her cheeks and into her hair, sending tingles across her scalp. "I like you. I more than like you." He skimmed his lips on hers, the lightest kiss that wasn't anywhere near what she craved. Then, he held her against his chest, and his heart thumped in her ear. "It's so good to hold you. I thought... I wondered if it would be different. If you would be or I would be or..." He leaned back and looked down at her, eyes narrowed. "Maybe I shouldn't have said that."

"I'm pro-honesty."

His lips tipped up at the corners, and though it was barely a smile, she realized it was the first she'd seen from him in a long time.

"It's just that we knew each other such a short time before I deployed, and then..." His words trailed, and dark scenes played across his face. There had already been so much about this man she didn't know, and now he'd been to war, a whole world she wouldn't understand even if he did open up to her.

But, for all her talk of being pro-honesty, there was a lot in her past he didn't know, either, and she wasn't about to tell him. As much as she wanted to know all of his secrets, she was hanging onto her own.

He'd called her innocent.

What would he think of her if he knew the truth?

In his expression, she saw wariness—or was it fear?

She had a million questions, but the important ones had been answered that November weekend eighteen months before. She gripped his hand, tapping his duffel bag with her toe. After he picked it up, she started walking again. They stepped outside into the warm afternoon—he let go of her hand long enough to put his hat on—and crossed the busy loading zones to the parking garage. "I figured you'd decide you could do better than a lowly chef."

"Lowly?" He chuckled. "Try talented. And kind. And generous. You're lovely, not lowly."

A blush warmed her cheeks. "Well, at work, I'm as lowly as can be." Not that she wanted to talk about her job. And he didn't want to talk about his mother, obviously. Now that Amanda had grown accustomed to his presence again, she saw things she hadn't noticed at first. Beyond his tan, he seemed pale. And though he'd put on muscle, he looked drawn. Dark smudges below his brown eyes told her he hadn't slept much on the long trip—or maybe in days. "How was your flight?"

"Uneventful." But at the thought of it, he rubbed his shoulder.

"Are you in pain?"

"No." He dropped his hand, looking around at the rows of cars. "What section?"

"I know where I'm going." They took the elevator, and she led the way to the proper aisle. "Your shoulder? That's what was injured?"

"It's fine."

She stifled a sigh. She could drop it, but how many subjects were going to be off-limits? "It's a simple question, Mark."

He shot her a look, lips flattened in a smirk. "Yes, my shoulder."

"What happened?"

"It's a long story."

She stopped to face him, crossing her arms. "Are we together, or aren't we?"

He blinked. "We are. I mean, aren't we?"

"You were injured badly enough that they sent you home. I think you could spare a couple of words to tell me what happened. Or at least in what way you were hurt. Were you shot?" He shook his head, but by the way his lips were pressed closed, had no intention of elaborating. "Step on a landmine? Trip over a tree trunk? Slip on a banana peel?"

That brought only the slightest quirk of his lips.

"I don't need the whole novel. Summarize."

"Fine." He hitched his duffel higher on his uninjured shoulder. "I had a run-in—a slight run-in... It was no big deal. It was just a local and a little...knife."

"A knife?" Her volume rose, the words pitched too high. "Someone stabbed you?"

"It's fine, Amanda. I'm fine."

"You were stabbed." Maybe if she kept saying it, the words would penetrate.

"It's okay." He pulled her close.

She squeezed his shirt in her fists, then loosened her grip for fear of hurting him, which didn't make any sense at all.

"This is why I didn't want to tell you."

"No, you have to tell me." She hadn't realized she was crying until she heard tears in her voice. "I'm sorry. I can handle it. Really, I can." She sniffed and swallowed a sob and stepped back. "I'm okay. It just surprised me, that's all.

Anything serious?" She swiped her eyes and shook her head. "Stupid question. You were stabbed. Of course it was..." She looked at his shoulder as if she could see past the thick fabric of his shirt.

"I'll show you, if you want to see it." Raising his eyebrows, he took a pointed look around the parking garage. "I'd rather not disrobe in public. Can it wait?"

"Of course. But it's...?"

"Just skin and muscle. The wound was deep, which is why they're making me take so much time to recover. I'll do a little PT. It'll heal. Nothing to worry about."

"But the person who did it... How did he get so close? How did it happen?"

Mark started walking again, though he'd never seen the car her parents had bought her for graduation. "We were in a village. Someone pretended to be friendly. The knife came out of nowhere."

It was obviously a long story, and he hadn't shared the half of it. When they reached her little hatchback, she unlocked the doors.

He tossed his bag in the backseat and held out his palm. "You want me to drive?"

"Not unless you want to."

"I'm exhausted, so if you don't mind—"

"I got it. Climb in."

He folded his oversize body into her tiny car, pushing the seat back as far as it would go and then reclining it.

She maneuvered out of the garage and through the busy airport traffic toward Route One. The steakhouse wasn't far, and she'd mapped the route before she'd left that morning.

Mark was quiet beside her. At a light, she glanced at him

and saw he'd fallen asleep. The peace in the set of his lips and around his eyes highlighted how anxious he'd been before.

It said something that he knew she was safe, that he could relax in her presence. She wished she could relax as well.

But the man she loved had been stabbed, and in two weeks, he'd return to a war zone.

In twenty minutes, she'd have to endure a meal with his mother, who'd decided she hated her before she'd even met her.

And...who was Annalise?

MARK'S MOTHER had chosen a high-priced steakhouse, then complained about the food, the ambiance, and the service.

Amanda knew the restaurant industry and thought maybe they could connect on that subject, but when she tried to engage with her, Mrs. Johnson looked down her nose as if she were as second rate as the establishment.

"I'm sure you've been to some lovely little places down in...where is it you live again?"

"Providence." Did Amanda's smile look as fake as it felt? She was glad the table separated her from Mark's parents—and that he sat right beside her. "But I grew up west of Boston."

His mother named the more crime-ridden neighborhoods near the city. "Plenty of *authentic* options." She added the last with a curled lip.

Amanda ignored the digs. "I do love cuisine from all over the world."

"Amanda's from Natick, Mom." Mark found her hand on

the booth they shared and held it. "It's not exactly the inner city."

Amanda kept her press-on smile in place. "I know food because I'm a chef."

"And a very talented one," Mark added.

Mrs. Johnson dabbed the corners of her lips with her napkin, then folded it on her lap before aiming her gaze at her son. "You know this how? She's cooked a lot of meals for you?"

"She cooked for me, yeah."

Amanda was glad Mark didn't share which meal. Telling her Amanda had made him breakfast would have only confirmed what she already believed.

"I also watched her teach kids to bake biscuits and croissants."

She faced him, flushing with pleasure. "I forgot you were there."

"They smelled great." He directed his words at his mother. "I didn't taste them, but she sent me boxes of the most delicious homemade candy and fudge."

The woman's face turned a very unattractive shade of red.

Mark either didn't notice or pretended not to as he kissed Amanda's temple. "She's always sending me things. Her parents too." To Amanda, he said, "Did you know they send me something every week? Letters, cards, care packages. The guys hang around my bunk at mail call, just in case one of you sends me food. Your family is the reason I have so many buddies."

"That and your winning personality."

"That too." He spoke to his father, taking on a more

serious tone. "I devour your letters. They remind me I'm not alone."

"The Lord is with you, son, and you're never far from our thoughts."

*Our?*

Amanda thought Hayden was generous to include his wife in that statement.

"Well." Mrs. Johnson cut a bite of her steak. "None of it would be necessary if you'd just gone to Princeton like I told you to."

Hayden sent his wife a warning look. "Mark gets to choose his own path."

"Don't worry about it, Dad. It's not like it's a newsflash. She doesn't exactly hold her opinions close."

"You're both being ridiculous." The woman dropped her fork with a clatter. "I'm only stating the obvious. You can't be happy you've gone to war. And you"—she glared at her husband—"pushing him to put his life in danger. What kind of father does that?"

"I didn't push him. I told him to do what he felt called to do. I served. There's honor serving your country."

"Oh, please." Her predator eyes homed in on Amanda. "And you. I bet you love telling people your boyfriend's a Marine."

Amanda's spine stiffened, her heart hammering with outrage. "You don't know me. You don't know anything about me."

"I know your kind."

"My kind? What kind is that?"

"The kind that tricks a foolish man into thinking he's in love in three days with false-innocence and lash-flapping.

Where'd you learn those skills? Not in community college or chef school, that's for sure."

"That's enough, Mother." Mark shoved out of the booth and held out his hand to Amanda. "Let's go."

She took it, slid to the edge, and let him pull her to her feet.

"Sorry, Dad, but I can't... I just can't."

"I understand, son." Hayden's expression wasn't disappointed but resigned. Apparently, his wife's behavior didn't surprise him at all.

What was wrong with her?

When Mark tried to tug Amanda away, she didn't budge, looking down at the woman who'd looked down on her all day. "Your son is the most amazing, most wonderful, most courageous man I've ever known, and you don't even see it. Am I happy he went to Afghanistan?" Her volume rose, but she didn't soften it. "Am I happy that he's going back? Obviously not. But am I proud of him?" She let the question hang there, giving the woman a moment to say something, anything.

But Patricia Johnson was silent.

"What rational person wouldn't be proud?" Amanda finally asked. "Of course I'm proud of Mark. Your son...my boyfriend, is a hero."

"Yeah!" The word came from somewhere behind her.

Suddenly, people applauded.

Mrs. Johnson's face flushed.

Mark groaned, dropping his head and rubbing the back of his neck.

Maybe she'd embarrassed him, but he was a hero, and the world should know it.

Amanda leaned down and spoke just loudly enough for the horrible woman to hear. "You know nothing about me. But after this meal, I know you. You're a fool, and you're missing the best thing in your life."

She straightened and looked at Hayden, whose eyes were wide with shock. "Thank you for lunch."

"It's been"—his lips tipped up in the barest smile—"a pleasure."

Patricia was spluttering at her husband, but Amanda paid her no attention as she turned and walked beside Mark.

The sound of applause followed them to the exit.


AMANDA WAS TREMBLING—WITH rage or victory, she wasn't sure. She drove east, unsure where she should go, where Mark wanted her to take him. Much as she'd like to, she didn't think she ought to head south to Rhode Island, considering his parents lived north in New Hampshire.

They needed to think and regroup and breathe.

Was he mad at her? He hadn't said a word since they'd left the restaurant. At a straightaway on the winding two-lane road, she shot a look in his direction.

He was smiling. "That was amazing. I am worried, though."

"I'm sorry. I shouldn't have—"

"I thought you were smarter than that."

Fear sent acid to her stomach. "You're right. I should've—"

"A smarter woman would've run screaming, leaving my mother—and me—far behind."

She opened her mouth to apologize again, then changed tack. "You're messing with me? Now?"

"Do you have any survival instincts at all?"

Amanda chuckled, the sound as lighthearted as it was shocking, considering the circumstances. "You know your mom better than I do. What do you think? Does she like me?"

He barked a laugh. "I can't believe you did that. You called me courageous? That was awe-inspiring. I've seen grown men cower at weaker attacks."

She would've cowered, too, if the dragon lady had satisfied herself by criticizing Amanda. But the way the woman had ripped into Mark was unacceptable.

Now that there were some miles between them, though... She groaned.

What had she done? She didn't make scenes. She didn't stand up to bullies or didn't call people on their nonsense. She brushed people's stuff under the rug and served them cookies. That was Amanda's MO.

"Is that the ocean?" Mark peered between two buildings at the expanse of water, sounding impressed all over again. "Good navigating, sweetheart. Pull in up there." He pointed to a lot, and she found a spot overlooking Revere Beach. Though a few puffy clouds floated overhead, the sky was mostly blue, the air in the seventies.

After she parked, she left her hands on the wheel and breathed, trying to come to terms with what had happened.

"I can see what you're doing, and you need to stop." Before she could argue, Mark hopped out, rounded the car, and opened her door. "Come on." He helped her out, then pulled her in for a hug.

Pressed against his chest, the argument with his mother

floated away on the sea breeze. Amanda wrapped her arms around his neck and held on. She inhaled his scent, now mixed with brine and exhaust from the passing cars. Waves crashed against the shore, but she focused on the beating of Mark's heart and the feel of his warm breath in her hair.

They didn't move for a long, long time.

"This is all I wanted." His words rumbled. "This is why I came home."

"I thought your CO insisted."

She shouldn't have said that. At the accusation in her tone, she expected him to go still or get annoyed, but he chuckled.

"You met my mother. Would you want to go home to her?"

Good point. He could come home to Amanda, but they weren't married, and he refused to stay at her apartment with her.

Mark was old-fashioned about such things. She'd minded until he'd explained that he intended to honor her—that she was worth waiting for.

Sweet. But his ideals were keeping them apart, and she didn't like that one bit.

And he'd be going home to his parents' house, and it wasn't like she'd be invited there to visit. "I wanted your mother to like me."

"That was never going to happen."

She leaned back. "Am I so unlikable?"

He smirked. "Yeah, that's the problem. That's why I love you, because you're unlikable."

"I'm serious. What did I do wrong?"

"Are you rich? Famous? Connected?" His eyebrows

hiked. "Can you get her into the right country clubs or introduce her to powerful people?"

"She doesn't know I can't."

"She would assume because I chose you, and that's not the kind of woman I would choose. Or, let me put that differently. If that were the kind of woman I'd chosen, I'd have told her so she would like you. Or she thinks I would have, anyway. She thinks everyone values the same shallow things she values."

"So there was never a chance?"

He exhaled, shaking his head. "I guess, if you were the boot-licking sort. But I don't like to kiss boot-lickers. Bad breath."

She smiled at his attempt at humor. "Which was Annalise, then? Rich and famous, or a bootlicker?"

Mark's expression darkened like someone had shut off the light. He stepped back. "Who told you about Annalise?"

She explained how she'd overheard his parents talking at the airport, and the more she talked, the darker his expression became. By the time she was done, his shoulders were hunched, and his head hung low.

"I'm lucky you didn't run screaming before I got off the plane."

"I'm not going anywhere. You're worth whatever your mother throws at me. It's just that I wondered who Annalise is, that's all. Especially when your father seemed..." Amanda wasn't sure how to explain what she'd heard—or hadn't heard. "He said you'd made your choice, but it didn't sound like he thought you'd made the right choice, if that makes sense."

Mark leaned against the hood of her car, facing the ocean.

He wrapped one arm around her, and she nestled in beside him.

"I dated Annalise in high school. She wasn't any of those things I said—rich or famous or connected. Her family immigrated from Germany, and she was awkward, sort of a fish out of water. She used to ask my mother a million questions about everything you can imagine. Where to shop, how to dress, how to organize an event, how to host a dinner party. She wasn't a boot-licker, but she adored my mom, which, of course, convinced Mom she was brilliant. Annalise just wanted to fit in, and she didn't have anybody else to ask. She didn't have a lot of friends."

"Why not?"

He glanced at Amanda. "She was...is very attractive. The guys were too intimidated to ask her out, and the girls apparently didn't want to be friends with her for the same reason. I only got to know her because I was assigned to be her partner on a project in school. We became friends and then started dating."

"It was serious."

"Yup."

"What happened?"

"We graduated. She went to New York to pursue her dream, and I went to the Naval Academy."

"What was her dream?"

He rubbed his lips together. "To become a model."

"Oh. Tough business." Amanda could picture a gorgeous blonde with the same name who'd been on covers of every fashion magazine imaginable for years. "Funny. She has the same name as that supermodel..."

It was the way he cringed.

And the worry he'd shown from the moment Amanda had mentioned his ex's name.

"Don't tell me. You dated *her*? The supermodel?"

He pushed off the car and faced Amanda. "She was just a girl, sweet and funny and down-to-earth. She's none of those things anymore. Now, she's everything my mother wants for me. She's rich and superficial and has all the connections Mom wants."

"She's perfect."

"She has nothing I want." Mark took Amanda's hands. "You're who I want."

"Right." Until Annalise came knocking. And then what would happen?

"This." He pulled Amanda close and dipped his head, kissing her neck, her cheek. "This is what I want."

How was she supposed to think when he did that? Maybe, finally, he'd kiss her for real.

"But what if she decides she wants you?" Her voice sounded breathy and weak.

He sighed and leaned back. "She's reached out a few times."

"What?" Amanda stepped back. "When?"

"Before I met you. I'm not interested in her or her lifestyle, and she's not interested in mine."

"But maybe she'll decide—"

"Amanda." He gripped her shoulders gently and bent to look into her eyes, holding her gaze. "I love you. Her paper-thin looks do not compare to your beauty. She was my past. You're my future. That is, if you don't let minor wounds and airbrushed models and cruel mothers scare you away." He raised one eyebrow over his gorgeous eyes. "I might be the

Marine, but you're the one taking all the risks. Are you brave enough to stick with me?"

Was she?

There were so many things that could go wrong. But this man was worth every battle she'd have to endure. She slid her hands up his broad chest and around his neck. "Under one condition."

"Anything."

"I'm going to need a kiss, and not like the ones you've been giving me. A proper kiss, like you mean it."

"Oh? I think I can make that happen." His lips met hers, and she opened up to this man she loved with all her heart.

And welcomed him home.

The End...for now.

But Amanda and Mark's story continues, and just like in real life, there is no such thing as a trouble-free "happily ever after" life, not if people live very long.

Especially not when there are secrets involved. And unfortunately, Mark and Amanda are both keeping a few secrets.

You're not going to want to miss *Finding Amanda*, book 2 in the Amanda series. The expanded edition—including all-new bonus content—releases October 8.

Turn the page for more about *Finding Amanda*.

# ABOUT FINDING AMANDA:
## EXPANDED EDITION

**An award-winning novel with brand-new bonus content...**

Amanda Johnson hopes that publishing her memoir will finally bring justice to the psychiatrist who abused her as a teenager and heal the wounds that have long festered. But her estranged husband, Mark, is determined to talk her out of exposing her traumatic past.

A former marine, Mark's instincts for danger have never steered him wrong, and he's convinced the abusive psychiatrist is more than just a predator—he's a full-blown psychopath. Yet now that Mark and Amanda are separated, she no longer trusts his judgment or welcomes his protection.

When a stranger intervenes to shield Amanda from her abuser, Mark faces a new battle. Now he must safeguard Amanda both from the charmer who threatens their marriage and the psychopath who threatens her life.

**From a USA Today bestselling author... Don't miss this gripping tale of trauma, justice, and the extraordinary strength of a man who'll do anything to protect the woman he loves.**

ALSO BY ROBIN PATCHEN

The Wright Heroes of Maine

Running to You

Rescuing You

Finding You

Sheltering You

The Coventry Saga

Glimmer in the Darkness

Tides of Duplicity

Betrayal of Genius

Traces of Virtue

Touch of Innocence

Inheritance of Secrets

Lineage of Corruption

Wreathed in Disgrace

Courage in the Shadows

Vengeance in the Mist

A Mountain Too Steep

The Nutfield Saga

Convenient Lies

Twisted Lies

Generous Lies

Innocent Lies

Beautiful Lies

Legacy Rejected

Legacy Restored

Legacy Reclaimed

Legacy Redeemed

Christmas in Nutfield — November, 2024


Amanda Series

Chasing Amanda

Finding Amanda

# ABOUT THE AUTHOR

Robin Patchen is a *USA Today* bestselling and award-winning author of Christian romantic suspense. She grew up in a small town in New Hampshire, the setting of her Nutfield Saga books, and then headed to Boston to earn a journalism degree. After college, working in marketing and public relations, she discovered how much she loathed the nine-to-five ball and chain. After relocating to the Southwest, she started writing her first novel while she homeschooled her three children. The novel was dreadful, but her passion for storytelling didn't wane. Thankfully, as her children grew, so did her writing ability. Now that her kids are adults, she has more time to play with the lives of fictional heroes and heroines, wreaking havoc and working magic to give her characters happy endings. When she's not writing, she's editing or reading, proving that most of her life revolves around the twenty-six letters of the alphabet. Visit robinpatchen.com/

subscribe to receive a free book and stay informed about Robin's latest projects.

subscribe to receive a free book and stay informed about Robin's latest projects.

www.ingramcontent.com/pod-product-compliance
Lightning Source LLC
Chambersburg PA
CBHW071937190726
48293CB00004B/1272